Starting Over
Jordan Silver

COMING SOON
Seal Team Seven Book 6

Discover other titles by Jordan Silver

SEAL Team Series
Connor
Logan
Zak
Tyler
Cord

The Lyon Series
Lyon's Crew
Lyon's Angel
Lyon's Way
Lyon's Heart
Lyon's Family

Passion
Passion
Rebound

The Pregnancy Series
His One Sweet Thing
The Sweetest Revenge
Sweet Redemption

The Spitfire Series
Mouth
Lady Boss
Beautiful Assassin

The Protectors
The Guardian
The Hit Man
Anarchist
Season One
Season Two

Eden High
Season One
Season 2

What A Girl Wants
Taken
Bred

Sex And Marriage
My Best Friend's Daughter
Loving My Best Friend's Daughter

The Bad Boy Series
The Thug
Bastard
The Killer
The Villain
The Champ

The Mancini Way

Catch Me if You Can
Hold Me If You Can

The Bad Girls Series
The Temptress
The Seductress

Other Titles by Jordan Silver
His Wants (A Prequel)
Taking What He Wants
Stolen
The Brit
The Homecoming
The Soccer Mom's Bad Boy
The Daughter In Law
Southern Heat
His Secret Child
Betrayed
Night Visits
The Soldier's Lady
Billionaire's Fetish
Rough Riders
Stryker
Caleb's Blessing
The Claiming
Man of Steel
Fervor
My Little Book of Erotic Tales
Tryst
His Xmas Surprise

Tease
Brett's Little Headaches
Strangers in The Night
My Little Farm Girl
The Bad Boys of Capitol Hill
Bad Boy
The Billionaire and The Pop Star
Gabriel's Promise
Kicking and Screaming
His Holiday Gift
Diary of a Pissed Off Wife
The Crush
The Gambler
Sassy Curves
Dangerously In Love
The Billionaire
The Third Wife
Talon's Heart
Naughty Neighbors
Forbidden
Deception
Texas Hellion
Illicit
Queen of My Heart
The Wives
Biker's Baby Girl
Broken
Indiscretion
The Good Girl
The Forever Girl
Biker's Law

Bad Santa
Redneck
Savage
My Ward My Woman

Jordan Silver Writing as Jasmine Starr
The Purrfect Pet Series
Pet
Training His Pet
His Submissive Pet
Breeding His Pet

Writing as Tiffany Lordes
American Gangster
Double The Trouble

License Notes

All Rights Reserved. In accordance with the U.S Copyright Act of 1976, the scanning, uploading, and electronic sharing of any part of this book without the permission of the publisher/author is unlawful piracy and theft of the author's intellectual property. Thank you for your support of the author's rights.

This book is a work of fiction. Names, characters, places and incidents are the product of the author's imagination or are used fictitiously. Any resemblance to actual events, locales, or persons, living or dead, is coincidental.

Copyright © 2017 Jordan Silver

First eBook edition: April 2017

Chapter 1
JULIE
***

Starting over. Who knew it could be such a pain in the ass? One minute it feels like the world is your oyster and there're a million roads you can take. And the next, the fear threatens to choke the life out of you because you're a thirty one year old woman with two kids and no prospects for anything even resembling a future.

If not for my kids, I just might take a long walk off the proverbial short pier. But the thought of leaving my poor babies alone in the world that had shown me nothing but all the ugliness it has to offer, makes me ill.

I got lost in my head for a minute as I looked unseeingly out the window. Sugar Creek had changed a lot since I left. The town was a mix of ranchers and bikers but where once there was a bit of a divide between the two, everything seemed to be blending together these days. A lot of the guys around here were ex military and these days that laid back feel I'd known as a child had a bit of an edge to it.

It had been ten years and a lot can happen in ten years, but somehow I never imagined I'd see the day when bikers and ranchers mingled together down Main Street. Even the shops had changed over time. Now instead of just the feed store and the grocers, and other ranching supplies establishments, there were bike shops and tattoo parlors mixed in.

You were just as likely to see a cowboy with spurs walking down the sidewalk, as you were a biker in his leathers and the sound of a hog or two tearing through town. I shook off my daydreaming and finished getting ready.

"Tiana, quit it and get down from there before you break your neck." I pulled at the strap of my loose bra for the one hundredth time without much luck of making it do what I want, while trying to stop my youngest from falling over the back of the ratty old chair in the shabby room of the rundown motel, which is all I can afford until the lawyers straighten things out in the divorce.

10 STARTING OVER

"Dylan, get over here and help me with your sister please." I wasn't looking forward to the look on his face when he dragged himself from in front of the TV to do my bidding. Since the split he's been getting worse and I'm running out of options. Short of dropping him off at his dad's door, which is what he keeps screaming is his greatest wish, there isn't much I can do to make his life easier.

My seven year old who was being made to grow up way too fast flounced himself off the bed and made his way over to my four year old who, bless her heart had no idea that her life had changed for the worse. At least there was that.

Dylan, because he was older and was at that age where he knew more, felt the brunt of the mess that I'd made of my life. While his sister was still too young to grasp anything more than the fact that she was no longer going to bed at night in the princess room mommy and daddy had made for her.

"I don't see why I have to watch her, I'm just a kid you know." I'd been hearing those words more and more often in the last few days since my once carefree little boy had been dragged away from his life of ease to…this.

I called myself a fool for the one-hundredth time since our world had been turned topsy-turvy, but there was no use. Feeling sorry for myself, and questioning the decisions I'd made ten years ago when I was too young and stupid to listen to the guidance of people who knew better wasn't going to put food on the table.

"The sitter will be here any minute and then you can go back to your show." I felt that hollowness in my gut, the one that has been a constant companion in the last few weeks. I am a horrible mom. I'd spent the first years of their lives not letting them spend too much time in front of the set and now I'm letting the damn thing practically raise them.

It couldn't be helped now though, and as soon as I got back on my feet things were sure to go back to the way they used to be. The knock at the door alerted me to Tracy's arrival and I rushed to answer while trying to put an earring and a shoe on at the same time.

1 | STARTING OVER
2

"Hi Ms. Julie, sorry I'm late mom had to get gas." The teen bounced into the room with all the glow of blossoming youth and dropped her bag and books on the wobbling table near the window. "Oh you're fine sweetie. Do you remember where everything is?" It would be hard not to, seeing as you can take the whole room in at a glance.

Her nod as she walked over to Tiana with a smile eased the knot in my gut. Tracy is the stepdaughter of my oldest and dearest friend. The only person who'd stood by me through all this, and one of the first I'd dropped at the behest of my husband when he was segregating me from everyone and everything I knew in the beginning.

"I'll be home by eleven, thank you so much for doing this." She waved me off as I kissed my babies goodbye and headed out the door to my new job. There was a mixture of fear and excitement beating away in my chest as I climbed into my car.

As I looked out the rolled down window at the scenery as I drove by, I felt a lot better. I guess it was being shut up in that stuffy room all day that was adding to my melancholy. Shit, I'm gonna have to get the kids out more then, because if it could affect me like this who knows what it was doing to them.

There was no pool for them to play in like back home, no wide open yard with swings and no room packed with toys to keep them happy. I had to keep reminding myself that, I would get it all back one day. It might not be the same, but if I can just keep it together I can give them at least some of what they once had.

There were times I wanted to give in, to just turn around and go back to the life I'd walked away from. But then I'd remember the beatings and the put downs and what that would mean to my kids who were now getting too old not to know what was going on any longer, and that gave me the strength I needed to put one foot in front of the other and run hard in the opposite direction.

STARTING OVER

I looked down at the expanse of leg that showed above my knee and swallowed hard. It had been a while since I'd worn anything this risqué and I was feeling a bit self-conscious. My body wasn't what it used to be before I got married and had two kids, but I was still proud of it.

That may be the one thing I could thank my soon to be ex for. Because of his incessant put downs and criticism I'd struggled to keep my weight down after each pregnancy. I pushed him out of my mind since I didn't want to give him even that much, the son of a bitch.

***

It was three o'clock in the evening on a Wednesday and the place looked like it was already happening. I fought back the bile and uncertainty as I climbed out of my cluttered car. There was a line of bikes across one side of the lot and a few trucks scattered around. The windows were tinted, but the sign outside left no doubt as to what type of place this was.

I had Sandy to thank once again for this since it was her brother's place, Kevin. He was another worry I had to overcome, another embarrassment from the past. I hope like hell he isn't here tonight. I'm not quite ready to face him and see that look of 'I told you so.' Then again, if that's all I get it would be a minor miracle.

"Maybe this wasn't such a good idea after all." I tugged at my skirt and threw my bag over my shoulder with trepidation. I didn't even reach the door before the leers and catcalls begun as I hustled my way inside.

I searched the darkened interior for my friend who was the general manager of the restaurant and bar that was owned by her older brother. "Excuse me." I brushed by a bearded behemoth who was making his way to the bar.

"Whoa sweetheart, where did you come from?" I pulled my hand back and away from his grasp without daring a look at him as I made my way to the back where the offices were. Whatever possessed Sandy to think I could do this was beyond me.

Sure I needed the money since my ex had hidden his assets and I was damn near penniless, but she couldn't believe that I'd changed this much. This was way out of my comfort zone. The closest I'd ever come to a biker bar was on the screen.

Well Julie, you're just gonna have to pull up your big girl panties and do what you've got to. You have babies to feed and you damn sure need to get out of that hellhole. It wasn't that I wasn't qualified for anything else. I had a college degree after all. But it wasn't that easy landing a job when you'd done nothing with that degree since you got it. Not with jobs in such high demand and no real experience.

Chapter 2
JULIE
***

"Hey you made it. Did my little stinker get there on time?" I smiled fondly as she prattled on the way I remembered from our youth, answering her when she'd let me. All the while I kept an eye out for the last person I wanted to see today or any other day for that matter.

I'd spent the last ten years trying not to think of him, without much luck I might add, only to have him front and center in my mind every second these days. "You look spooked, look I told you, this job is easy. The crowd might be a little rough at times, but generally they're harmless. Tyson and his crew are on the door and trust me nothing goes on here that should make you afraid. Kevin runs a tight ship."

"He's here?" My pulse raced and my heart picked up speed in my chest. I'd be a liar if I said it was out of fear, though there was a bit of that. Her smirk didn't help.

"No, he's still on the job somewhere but he checks in as often as he can. Plus these guys are part of his team so they know what they're doing." His team. Last anyone knew Kevin was part of some military outfit that was more hush-hush than the Kremlin, but that was years ago, before things got even weirder. Now no one knew exactly what it was that he was a part of.

I'd lost touch with my old friend since a few weeks after the wedding because of Robert's bullshit which I can only see clearly now that the dust had cleared, so I wasn't too much in the know. But she'd been filling me in here lately since my return to the town where I'd grown up.

"I wish I'd never left." Where the hell did that come from? I hadn't meant to speak that truth out loud. "Well you're here now sweetie and we're gonna get you squared away before you know it." She walked over and wrapped her arms around me, something I didn't know I needed until she did it. I fought back the tears of self-pity as we broke the embrace. Now wasn't the time to fall apart.

"So, let me look at you in that uniform." She spread my arms open wide as she took in the short skirt and form fitting blouse that showed more skin than I was comfortable with. "You look great, now let me walk you through this again and you'll be good to go. By the way ignore the other girls they tend to be a bit catty with newcomers, pay them no mind."

"Anyone in particular?" The last thing I needed was to get caught up in female drama. I had enough on my plate thank you very much. "Natalie. She sees herself as the queen bee around here since Kevin made the monumental mistake of sleeping with her once long ago."

That hurt, but I knew my friend could have no idea how much. She didn't know the burning secret that I've been carrying for the past ten years. I hid my face under the pretense of checking my phone, but I was really just giving myself time for the blush to disappear from my cheeks.

"So are they a thing?" I couldn't help asking even though I made it seem like passing interest. Her snort assured me that it wasn't so. "Nah, though she'd give her eyeteeth to make that happen. No, I think it was more like a slip in judgment on his part, but she on the other hand seems to have fallen hard. It's been more than three years and she's still holding out hope. You shouldn't have a problem though since you're an old family friend, which they all have been made aware of."

If only she knew. I felt bad keeping something this big from her, but how the hell do I start that conversation? I'd already betrayed her so much by cutting her off all these years, how do I tell her that one of the reasons that had been so easy was because of what I'd done with her brother that long ago night?

The memory still had the power to make me uncomfortably hot and wracked with guilt. I was relieved when she changed the subject and moved onto something else. "I'll show you where to put your things, everyone gets a locker with their own lock so you can store your purse in there during your shift. I have you trailing Lucy, she's pretty good and one of the more even tempered girls. You'll be trailing for three nights until you get the hang of it, with pay, but you don't start making tips until you're officially on the floor."

"The place really picks up at around five and doesn't stop jumping until three in the morning, so you'll be run off your feet. But believe me, the money is good and Kevin pays his staff way above the national average, so we'll have you up and running in no time. I still wish you'd come and stay with Ron and me, we can certainly make room."

"Thanks but I can't put you out like that. I've been looking through the papers and there're a ton of places for rent. If the pay is as good as you say, I should be able to find something suitable before long."

STARTING OVER

If it were just myself I would've found something by now, but because Dylan had school and Tiana was going to be starting soon, I needed to find something close by. Plus I wanted the kids to have space and most of the places in the city didn't offer much of that.

"Suit yourself but you know the offer still stands." When she grew quiet I knew what was coming next. "So how are you really?" The rub to my shoulder offered comfort and it would've been so easy to fall into the woe is me mindset that I'd been nursing for so long now, but my past treatment of my good friend held me back.

"I'm okay, this was a long time coming. It's not like I'm overly surprised. I just feel bad for the kids you know. Especially Dylan. He misses his dad and does not understand why he can't have all the things he owned only a week ago." It's weird how that works. Robert never had time for his son but now that he was gone the boy seemed to have manufactured this alternate reality where he was the world's greatest dad. I know it had more to do with the things he once had, like a home, than anything else.

That still makes me feel like a failure, the fact that I couldn't take care of my kids in the same fashion, as their abusive dad. I questioned my decision to leave for the thousandth time and still came back to the same answer. It was the only thing I could've done. It was one thing for me to excuse away his horrible treatment of me, but when that brutality started shifting towards my kids it was time to go.

I rubbed my wrist where the phantom pain still lingered from the last time he'd snapped it like a twig....
"Okay I can see that mind of yours working, let's get you to work and your mind on better things to come."

***

I spent the first few hours looking over my shoulder expecting Kevin to show up any minute. After the obligatory hellos, Lucy took me under her wing and showed me the ropes. Once my fear was gone and I saw the way she handled the more over zealous patrons, I felt my unease relax more as the evening wore on. There was only one hiccup, and that came when I met Natalie.

If Sandy hadn't warned me I would've picked up on the other woman's hostility right off the bat. She looked me up and down when Lucy made the introductions and I wasn't sure if to be relieved, or insulted, when she dismissed me with a look.

I could see why Kevin had gone there; she was beautiful. Her blonde svelte looks begged the question of why she was wasting her time here when she could obviously do very well on any runway in the world.

I had no right, but I felt just a little bit jealous at the fact that she had once known him. I well remember what that feels like. Since that road led nowhere good, I quickly shook myself off and paid attention to what Lucy was showing me.

By the end of the night my feet were on fire and I felt like I'd been going for a week, but I did feel a great sense of accomplishment when the younger woman heaped praise on my head for the quick way in which I picked up everything.

"No, thank you for being so patient. I have a new respect for the job sheesh." We both laughed as we made our way back to the office so she could show me how to check out. The whole thing seemed simple enough and I wasn't so afraid of falling flat on my face anymore.

"Here, you rocked it tonight you deserve this." I stepped back and away from her with my hands up. "Oh no I couldn't. Sandy already explained that I don't start making tips until after my training."

"Take it, trust me, I wished my trainer had done the same for me because I really could've used it…not that you look like you're in need or anything." She rushed to add on, making me laugh.

"It's okay I didn't think you meant that. I appreciate it really, but you don't have to." Though the fifty she held out could be put to good use, I wasn't that desperate yet to take the poor girl's money. She'd told me her story throughout the night as I followed her from table to table.

She had a kid at home to feed and no husband. I couldn't in all good conscience take food from her son's mouth. She shrugged and put the money away with the rest of her tips which weren't too shabby for a night's pay, and that too helped ease the strain I'd been laboring under since this whole mess began.

Chapter 3
JULIE
***

We went to a different office from Sandy's where the night manager was busy watching the monitors, keeping an eye on the floor while doing paperwork. They both walked me through the checkout process, which was relatively painless.

After that I went in search of Sandy and knocked on her door. "It's open."
She smiled when she saw it was me. "So how was it? Come in, close the door." She swung around in her chair behind the desk as she ushered me into the room. It felt good to get off my feet, like I hadn't sat in forever. "It wasn't as bad as I feared and if I only have to do it four nights a week I think I'll be fine."

I knew I owed my old friend a hell of a lot after the shitty way I'd treated her in the past. All it had taken was one phone call. There were no questions, no recriminations. Just come on back and we'll take care of you. Not even my own family had been that welcoming.

"I told you. I did it for a while when Kev first opened the place so I knew you'd be fine. How were the guys? They weren't too assholish were they? I know some of them can be a bit much to take, but once you get used to it you'll see they're harmless."

"They were fine. Lucy played mama bear so that pretty much kept them in line." She was right, that was gonna take getting used to. After years of hiding in the shadows, being front and center was going to take some time.

Robert never liked me being around people, something I'd learned way too late along with a hell of a lot of other shortcomings that should've been huge warning signs. Just thinking about him brought that cold chill that ran down my spine more and more of late. That, and the reminder, that I had been a total and complete fool for the past ten years.

"You're doing it again." Sandy's voice pulled me back to the room where we sat. "Doing what?"

"Thinking about him. I always know when he steps into the room because you get this look on your face. I know I told you I wouldn't push, but maybe if you talked about it…"

I'd been putting this off for the past week or so since I moved back to my hometown but I knew the time would come when I'd have to share. I'm surprised she'd let me go this long without spilling, but maybe she was right. A quick look at my watch showed that I still had a half an hour before I had to go.

"I don't even know where to start." I hadn't talked about my life to anyone not even family members. I just never felt like anyone would listen. They'd all been so proud when I'd married Robert, even when I'd had doubts and my heart had been elsewhere...that's a whole other story, better leave that alone for now.

"Just start at the beginning. I don't know about you, but when I heard your voice on the phone it felt like the years had just melted away. It was like we were back in high school again; remember? We shared everything back then. There wasn't anything we didn't tell one another." Another lie I'm gonna have to live down, because there was one huge secret I hadn't told her and probably never would.

I took a deep breath before diving in. "Well, let's just say that the Robert you met is not the Robert I was married to for the last ten years." I shook my head at my own folly. She didn't say a word, just placed that finger of hers under her chin the way she always used to when she was paying attention and let me get my thoughts together.

"It started with little things you know. Don't wear this; don't talk to this person. Where are you going? Who was that on the phone? Then when I wanted to go to work that was a problem too, and stupid me I believed he just wanted to take care of me. I didn't see that he was trying to control me. You got any water in that fridge?" I pointed to the mini fridge in the corner and she rolled her chair over to get us both a bottle.

I took a deep swallow, the first in hours before continuing my story. "Anyway, I went along with everything because that's what I thought I was supposed to. Mom always deferred to dad and that's pretty much all I knew, so I didn't think too much of it at the time."

"Then the complaints started. The food wasn't good enough, or the house wasn't cleaned the way he liked. My hair wasn't just right. But I don't think even with all that that my eyes were opened until the day two weeks after I gave birth to Dylan when he called me fat. I'd only gained fifteen pounds with my pregnancy."

I accepted the look of distaste on her face, I've worn it a time or two myself when dealing with my soon to be ex. "Of course I stayed even as things got worse, even...even after the first time he hit me." I saw her body jerk as if taking a blow and bowed my head in shame at the sheen of tears in her eyes.

"He hit you? That weak son of a bitch, I ought to go find him and kick his ass." My loud bark of laughter broke the tension. Her reaction was just what I needed to ease the pressure in my chest; like old times. "Easy tiger, let's hope neither of us ever have to see him again." I told her about the restraining order I'd been forced to take out against the man I shared children with, and how hard that decision had been to make on my own.

I told her about the lies and heartache when the truth finally came out. The stares from the neighbors who'd suspected all along that my life was an unraveling lie but who'd been kept at a distance at my husband's behest and so had no way of letting me in on the secret.

"You know I still don't know if he kept me isolated so that I never found out the truth about him? Or if that's just the way he is. I just know that once the veil came off and the truth started flooding out I was at a loss. I never knew one person could keep so many secrets for so long. He even fooled my dad and that's something I would've never believed possible."

"So he wasn't a big shot exec after all?" I could well understand her look of confusion. "Oh no he was, but he was also doing some shady shit under the table which his bosses kept under wraps for fear of getting the company in trouble. It's all very confusing and by the time I found out what was going on I just wanted out of there anyway."

"I'd long lost whatever feelings I had for the man since like the first six months of marriage, so what he did or didn't do was no longer of any concern to me. I just worry about my kids. They love their dad and it would break my heart to take away that ideal they have of him. I don't think they'd understand anyway at their age, but I knew I couldn't stay."

"What about alimony, child support? Does he even still have a job?"

"Oh he does. His dad stepped in and cleaned up his mess, but he has to repay the money he stole or face a jail sentence. That's why it took the lawyer so long to work out some kind of payment deal. If it were up to Robert he wouldn't give us a dime. The house belonged to the company, something else I didn't know. He'd led me to believe it was a gift from his parents."

"Was anything about this guy even real?" I had to think about that one. Even as the humiliation beat strongly in my chest, I had to accept that I had made the biggest mistake of my life when I said 'I do' to that scum.

"His hair, he does have good hair." That was good for another laugh. But when I thought of what all I'd lost when I chose him, it made my heart hurt. Not that Kevin had offered marriage that night so long ago. And the reality was that I'd been purely selfish when I turned to him the night before walking down the aisle. It's as if I knew even back then that I didn't want to give the man my dad had chosen for me my most precious gift.

I have to stop thinking about this. It's in the past and I'm sure never to be revisited again. But from the moment I realized my marriage was over my mind has been filled with Kevin and that one night we'd shared. If I were honest it had started long before that. In fact, that night was never far from my thoughts. Something I used to feel horrible guilt over.

Chapter 4
JULIE
***

After I'd told my friend as much of the sordid details of my life I could stomach for one night it was time to head back to the depressing little room and the one thing I found pleasure in these days, my kids. As I got behind the wheel I took one last look in the mirror, stupidly hoping that somehow Kevin would be there, watching. It's a scene I've played out numerous times in the last few days.

Truth be told I'd been on pins and needles all night expecting him to walk in. The longing that I'd kept leashed all these years seemed boundless now that I was back here where it all happened. And though I expected him to be angry and hateful after the way I'd left things, my stupid heart couldn't wait for that first sight of him.

STARTING OVER

It had taken me this long to admit to myself that I was truly head over heels in love with him, always had been. What had started out as a teenage crush on my best friend's brother at age fifteen had blown into full-fledged love by the time I turned eighteen. Only the town's heartthrob had been way out of my league and had never given me the time of day.

Until that night ten and a half years ago, when in one moment of heated passion we'd given in. Or I'd seduced him more like. I still don't know what had come over me then. I just knew that I wanted Kevin Hunt to be the man to take my virginity.

I knew even as I gave myself to him that it would be a one-night stand. Not that I'd believed anything more would come of it. He was after all a few years older and much worldlier than I was. The fact that he'd even given in to me had been a surprise. But I still remember the way I'd felt that night. It was the one and only time I'd ever truly enjoyed the act of lovemaking.

That was something else that had fed my guilt and kept me entrapped in a loveless marriage. I'd felt that somehow I'd cheated Robert, and the fact that I'd compared his clumsy efforts to Kevin in my mind had filled me with shame.

I brushed my thoughts aside as my chest grew tight at the memories. Outside the streets were quiet this close to midnight. The sky was bright with stars and a three quarter moon and the air fresh and clean.

I felt a spurt of excitement unfurl in my belly as I felt real joy at being back here again. This was the one place I'd always felt safe. Robert had hated it, calling it a hick town. He much preferred big city life

But me, this was the place where I'd laid at night dreaming about a future. I'd never wanted anything more than a ranch like the one my parents owned, a husband and a bushel of kids to look after. Every time I thought of a husband Kevin's face popped into my head and I had to fight it back.

It was never going to happen now, none of it. I'd burnt my bridges when I snuck in and out of his bed without telling him the truth. Even now the thought of how I'd handled things made me sick to my stomach. But it had been my only chance. That night I knew that if I didn't have him then I'd never get the chance again.

I don't know where I'd got the nerve to approach him. It was my first real try at flirting. Even as I stood in front of him shaking like a leaf in the wind, my heart racing out of my chest, I'd expected him to rebuff me.

Why wouldn't he? He was the most handsome guy around for miles, maybe in this county and the next. I knew he had girlfriends coming and going because Sandy was always keeping me abreast even when we went to two separate colleges.

I'd even seen him making out with one of them once when we were kids. That night I'd cried myself to sleep. I saw the kind of woman he was attracted to and knew I'd never measure up to them. I wasn't blonde and built. At five one I barely reached his chest. The girl he'd had pinned against the side of his parents house with his hands and mouth all over her had to be at least five nine, more suited to his six three height.

But that night I'd thrown caution to the wind. There'd been a need in me that to this day I still don't understand, but I knew I had to give myself to him. If I couldn't have the dream at least I could have that for the rest of my life. And I was right.

After my marriage turned out to be a sham, the memory of that night had seen me through many a heartache. There were times after Robert had taken a hand or a fist to me that I'd lay in bed with tears silently running down my cheeks because I'd been forbidden to make a sound lest I alert the children, that I'd take out the memory of how it felt to have those big rough hands on me. Or his mouth...Have mercy.

Robert had hated that he couldn't get my body to respond to him. In the end he'd blamed my coldness on the reason for his affairs, though by then I knew he'd been screwing some girl at the office even before we were married and hadn't stopped after.

He'd die if he knew that the only time I ever did have those orgasms he was so pleased about was when I imagined that it was Kevin inside of me. I felt shame and guilt over that as well. But the third time he hit me for not being wet enough I'd caught on quick and learned to use my imagination.

Or that the few times I'd been the one to turn to him for sex were those times when my need for Kevin was so strong that it was either that or use my fingers to pleasure myself. Back then I'd been so confused and wracked with enormous guilt. Had I known that he was a snake I would've been long gone.

But it had taken ten years for me to build up the courage to even think about seriously leaving him. When I was finally able to turn the tables on him and his lies and deception, my first thought had been of Kevin.

Then reality set in and I knew that once again it was just a dream; one that would never come to pass, because I'd thrown it all away on a shiftless no-good bastard to please my dad. I knew enough about Kevin to know that he would never forgive me for using him that night.

Chapter 5
KEVIN
***

"Where is she?" I was sweaty, tired and mad as fuck. Instead of heading home for some much needed rest, I was here sniffing after her ass. I'd told myself ever since the phone call from my sister telling me that her old friend was moving back to town and needed a job, that I wouldn't give a fuck.

"Who?" I knew from the smirk on her face that she knew exactly who I was referring to. "Don't play games, Julia, where is she?" My beast was damn near off his leash and it wouldn't take much to push me over the edge.

"I knew it. I knew there was something going on between you two years ago and I was right."

"What could be going on? She was married and gone." We'd never talked about Julia since the last time we saw her at our family home. Everyone else had gone to her wedding the next day but I hadn't. I'd been too fucking mad back then to look at her without wringing her fucking lying neck.

She'd snuck out of my bed in the middle of the night like a thief and just disappeared, and I hadn't heard or seen her since. Not a fucking peep. Until now.

I didn't know the whole story but from what little I'd gathered it was enough to tell me she was back on my turf now and I mean to get my pound of flesh.

"So what happened with her and the hotshot?" I'd done my own research but knew there was always more. In my line of work I am paid to ferret out secrets. The world is full of them, but this shit had fallen into my lap in the middle of something and I hadn't had enough time to go deep. That will all change soon.

She still had that annoying nosey ass little sister look on her face, but I wasn't giving her anything so she opened up. I knew from experience that she wouldn't give me everything. From what I remember the two of them had been thick as thieves, always having each other's backs. I knew that because of our upbringing that my sister wouldn't betray her friend's confidence, unlike some people I know who didn't give a fuck.

She knew a little more than I did, but I left the room feeling there was something she wasn't telling me. If I were a vengeful fuck, I would gloat at the fact that the son of a bitch she'd thrown me over for had done her shitty, but I had more than enough to fuck with her for without stooping to that.

Over the years I'd gone over and over this shit in my head. The way shit had gone down between us wasn't exactly orthodox, but it still pissed me the fuck off that she'd left my bed and went off to marry someone else. We weren't in love, had never even shared so much as a kiss before the night we fell into bed together. But I woke up the next morning with questions, while it seemed she'd already had the answers.

Before that night Julia had been the cute little kid that was always hanging around my house with my pain in the ass sister. Then she'd grown into something else entirely, but I'd still had no real interest. Okay that's not exactly true. But whatever interest I had was passing because she was just too fucking young and nowhere near ready for the man I was.

My years away in the navy while the girls were growing up had kept me away from home a lot so I'd missed most of their teenage years. Of course whenever I thought of the two of them I still saw the two little miscreants who were always getting into shit and keeping my dad on his toes.

And that's why my first sight of her that night at the party my family had thrown for one of my many homecomings had thrown my ass for a loop. It had taken me a minute or two to process my body's reaction to her. I was thinking some very ungentlemanly things about my sister's little friend.

The once scrawny kid with the knobby knees, braces, eyes that were too big for her face and a head full of unruly hair had grown into a very well poised young lady, and she was fucking gorgeous.

I remember my eyes had followed her around the room as my dick throbbed in need. I'd just landed stateside and it had been a while since I'd fucked anything other than my hand. But there was something else going on with me that night. The attraction was hard and I'd tried putting it down to just me being hard up for some snatch.

"She's changed a lot hasn't she, son?" Dad came over to pass me a beer while the room was buzzing with friends and family doing their thing. I'd been caught staring, but it was too late to shift my focus and pretend I wasn't checking out her assets. Plus I was sure the look of hunger on my face was a dead giveaway as to what I was thinking.

"Yup, what the hell happened?" It was hard to look away but so as not to seem like a perv in front of my old man I forced myself. I had a good eight years on her I knew. And after the shit I'd been through in the last ten or so, I knew I was way beyond that in experience, but damn if she didn't make a man want.

The old man shrugged his shoulders. "Hell if I know. It's all I can do to keep the young men around here from her and your sister." Sandy had grown too in the time I'd been off protecting my country, but she was my sister. She's always gonna be that scrawny pain in the ass that was always getting into my shit. Though I could see the changes in her, they were nothing compared to her friend.

It wasn't that Julia had ever been ugly, just a little awkward I guess. But there's no way in hell I could've expected this. She was way over the age of consent, probably twenty-one like Sandy, fresh out of college. I wondered then if she'd done the usual college thing, like going wild her first time away from home.

There's no way she'd survived that shit with her cherry intact, not looking the way she did. Though I could still see that innocence about her, that body screamed 'come fuck me'. Legs, that went on forever and a rack that defied gravity. The shits were mouth watering.

I was a bit startled by the uneasy feeling I had at the thought of someone else covering her. Uneasy hell, I was jealous as fuck that someone else might've had her. Not a look I usually wear and not one I was prepared for. It just made me look at her even more and with new eyes. It wasn't easy for me to accept that I wanted my sister's friend. A girl I had watched grow up in some way over the years.

I clocked her the rest of the night and didn't miss the little secret looks she kept throwing my way when she thought I wasn't looking. I should've known better, should've walked away. But somehow that night, I couldn't, didn't.

I pulled into my garage and turned the truck and the memories off. I'd come a long way in the last ten years. I'd used my head and resources to build a better future for me, and my family. In the little town where we lived, my family had always been damn near at the wrong end of the totem pole.

Dad had done construction, while mom, cleaned people's homes to help when things were rough. That's one of the reasons the friendship that had formed between my sister and Julia who was from one of the town's wealthier families, had been such a surprise.

The two girls were as different as night and day. Sandy was the streetwise tomboy with a chip on her shoulder while Julia was the pampered princess of the country club set. I wasn't around them much back then, by the time they became pals I was already in the service trying to pave my way. But I heard the stories and in my rare trips back home had seen the bond the two girls shared.

I flicked on the kitchen light and headed for the fridge and a bottle of juice. I could go for a beer, but knew better. Not with her this close, and not with my mind where it's at.

"I'm coming for you legs." Shit. I already had a plan in place, but it needed tweaking a bit. There was no room for error, and yes I was running this shit like an Op. The only problem was I didn't know exactly where this shit was gonna end. One minute I see myself forgiving her after I fuck the shit out of her, maybe keeping her, and the next I see myself using her and walking the fuck away. I liked that one best.

I hated that she still had this kind of hold over me. Hated that I still wanted her no matter how much I tried convincing myself that it was just revenge I was after. Did she ever think of me, of that night? Or had she just put me out of her mind as easily as she'd crawled in and out of my bed. Fuck! The fuck I care.

I gave the house a walkthrough the way I do each time I come back from a long haul. After getting Sandy's call I'd put a rush on the job I was in the middle of just so I could get back here…to her. It wasn't like I was gonna punk out and fall right back in, no fucking way. This time I was going in with my eyes wide open.

1

She stole something from me that night. I'm not quite sure exactly what, but I know that after that, after having her, nothing had ever been the same. I was never the most trusting motherfucker in the world and after the number she did on me I became even worse. But she also spoiled me for other women.

My dick can get hard no problem, but the ride is not the same. My disdain for the opposite sex was at an all time high after she fucked me and married the next dick. I'm sure it had something to do with her wealth and my lack of. She'd treated me like the hired help that was good for a fuck but not to trot out in public.

It had taken me a long time to get over the shit she'd pulled, a long time and a lot of second-rate pussy. Now she was back on my turf and I'm about to show her who the fuck she'd fucked with. The fact that my cock has been in some state of hardness since I learned that she was back in Sugar Creek was of no fucking consequence whatsoever.

Once making sure things were in order, it was time to get down to business. I wanted to handle things just between us, I didn't need anyone else in my shit, least of all my nosy ass sister who had fallen right back in with her friend it seemed. I wasn't going to be that damn gullible. I might fuck her, but I'll be damned if I'm ever gonna trust her again.

I shed my shirt and boots and dropped across the bed with my arms beneath my head. I wasn't going to bring her here which had been my original thought. I didn't want her in my space. I own a few rentals; one of them would be more than adequate.

Then there were the kids. I gritted my teeth at the betrayal and breathed through it. Over the years I'd avoided any kind of mention of her. Whenever my mind would go there I'd force that shit back. Even though I knew her life had moved on and that she most likely did have kids with this man. And why the fuck that should bother me so much was a mystery.

Whatever! They exist. I'll try to keep them out of the line of fire. Then there's the asshole she left me...no that's not quite right. We weren't exactly a 'thing', and that's the conundrum. That's the fuckery that leaves my gut twisted in knots. Where I'd woken up the morning after with semi-dreams of what could be playing around in my head, she'd just moved the fuck on.

It didn't take me long to realize what had happened after I'd searched my parents house thinking maybe she'd gone to Sandy's room so no one would know we'd fucked. Imagine my surprise when I found my family getting ready for her fucking wedding. She'd blindsided me and now it was my turn.

Was I being unfair? Fuck no. Had the tables been turned I'd be looked at like the worse kind of scum, why the fuck should she get away with that shit because she wears a skirt?

I was still a little murky on the details. I didn't even know at the time that she was engaged. I never would've touched her if I had. It was only after the nuptials that I picked up bits and pieces from my sister in passing and I learned that the skell had been hand picked by her dad.

The question of 'why' plagued me for months after that. Why the fuck had she slipped her ass into my bed if she knew this guy was on the horizon? That feeling of inadequacy, of not matching up did not sit well with me. It didn't then, and it sure as fuck doesn't now.

I'd beaten myself up for way too long over that shit, before I'd had to burn it out of my head. After that the anger had only grown into hate. I hated her until I wanted to erase her completely. In the beginning I'd done that by screwing everything that came my way, stupid. As time went on and I threw myself into my duties, it lessened. But always it lurked in the very recesses of my mind.

Now she was just where I needed her to be, at my mercy. Of course I'd given her a job. Once my sister had called it was all I could do not to jump on a plane home. But my years of training had taught me patience. I was no longer the twenty-nine year old bleeding heart. I had grown into the hardened fuck that the world cut a wide path around when they saw me coming.

Rolling over I hopped off the bed and went to grab a shower. Under the spray of the hot water I let my mind go over the details. I wasn't going to show my hand too early in the game. My aim is to reel her in just the way she'd done to me. Then when she least expects it, I'll spring the trap and give her a dose of her own damn medicine.

Chapter 6
JULIE
***

I rolled out of bed the next morning after another restless night. Just as I had the past few days, I started the day feeling like a crappy mom for having brought my kids to this. Looking over at the bed where they still slept, I felt that little tear in my heart widen. My poor babies! How am I ever going to make this right?

After a solid half an hour of feeling sorry for myself, it was time to get the day started. Thankfully school was out for the summer, which was a blessing, and a curse. It meant I had to find things for them to do during the day before heading to work at night.

My feet still hurt a little but nothing I couldn't handle, and with the first night out of the way I was no longer so wary of my new profession. Other than having to deal with my ex to finalize things in the near future, there was only one grey cloud hanging over my head; that first meeting with Kevin. I looked forward to it as much as I dreaded it.

"Put it away Julie." He probably hasn't given that night a second thought in all these years. I blotted the excess water from my face and made my way to the coffeepot. The kids wouldn't stir until after the first cup, but instead of looking forward to the peace and quiet that would afford, I dreaded instead the extra time it would give me to dwell.

***

"Come on sleepy heads time to wake up." I shook them under the covers before crawling in with them the way I did at home.
For the first few minutes we tickled and played like old times, before reality set in, before my little boy was reminded that this wasn't exactly the way things use to be. Here he had to share, not only a room but also a bed with his little sister, where before he had his own. I saw the change, the veil that came over his eyes once his little mind cleared.

Pulling away he hopped off the bed and headed for the bathroom without so much as a hello. The smile was gone, and the set to his shoulders told me more than words just what kind of mood he was in. I had a sour feeling in the pit of my gut as I watched with my baby girl held closely in my arms.

He was so much like his dad; had always looked up to him. My worry was that if I didn't handle this situation the right way, he too might grow into a self-entitled, selfish human being; something that would break my heart.

Putting the worry away I patted my daughter's shoulder and got her out of bed. "As soon as your brother's done go wash up and we'll have some cereal." There was a diner across the lot that we could go to for breakfast for a change, but I wasn't quite ready for that.

When I'd left this place years ago I had no idea that I would be leaving it behind for good. I'd imagined weekends and holidays spent here with the friends and family I'd known all my life. Robert had made it clear from day one that that wasn't going to happen.

I'd never even had a chance to say goodbye, and had only spoken to Sandy once or twice since the wedding, and we'd been so close before.

It broke my heart just a little that she'd accepted me back without question. Maybe if she'd lashed out at me when I first called this guilt wouldn't be as strong. But as the days go by I'm more and more convinced, that had the tables been turned, she would've never let it happen, she would've found a way.

I could only imagine the wagging tongues as soon as news spread that I was back, and honestly was not quite ready to face the music. I'm sure most people here probably expected me to become something, to make something of myself in all those years, but instead I return a failure.

The rest of the morning went pretty much as was to be expected. The kids whined and complained about their confined space while I did everything I could to settle them down. I looked out the dusty window at the parking lot. There was nowhere for them to go play and since I'd grown up here I knew it wasn't safe anyway; not in this part of town.

"You'll have a backyard again soon I promise, just give mommy a little time." What a failure. My little girl played on the floor with her doll while my son glared at me balefully. "You always say that. Why can't we go home? Daddy said..."

I wanted to yell at my son that I was tired to death of hearing those words, but my years of motherhood kicked in and I bit my tongue. I'd promised myself to shield them from as much of this misery as I could, yelling at him would achieve nothing but hurt feelings and even more uncertainty.

"I know Dylan, but daddy's not here, I am. Have I ever lied to you?" How do you reason with a seven year old who couldn't grasp the severity of the situation? How did I get through to him that the reason I'd made the decision I should've from the first year was because he'd seen his dad hit his mother?

That was the last thing I'd held onto, the fact that Robert kept his abuse well hidden. I was never hit in the face, not after that first time. The bruises were always well hidden under my clothes, except for those times he lost control and made my wrists black and blue. Then he'd forbid me to leave the house for fear of the neighbors guessing at his true nature. Couldn't have that.

I was such a damn fool, how had I endured that for even one second? I who had always sneered at the women on those TV shows, who made excuses for doing the same, had lived it. I guess that's why you should never judge.

Whatever! As dismal as outside looked, it was still a hundred times better than where we'd escaped from, whether my kids knew it now or not. Hopefully one day they'll understand.

I made myself busy with the kids so as to keep my mind off of things for a while, but nothing could keep my thoughts from straying to the one thing that had been plaguing me since my return.

As the time grew near for me to leave for the restaurant, the more nervous I became. I kissed my babies goodbye and though not as wary as the day before, there was still a gnawing feeling in the pit of my stomach. Would tonight be the night I see him? Or did he not even care that I was back?

Sandy had said that he was away on business but somehow I still got the feeling that he was going to show up any minute. Wishful thinking maybe? As I pulled into the parking lot I looked around even though I had no idea what kind of car or truck he drove. My walk to the entrance was pretty much the same as the day before with appreciative comments from patrons who were either coming or going. And then there was Tyson the head of security and a horrible flirt.

My face broke out in a smile at my first sight of him. "Well hey sugar, I see we didn't scare you off." His smile was open and friendly and I knew from Sandy and Lucy that he was a sweetheart. He'd grown up in Sugar Creek and had been in the service with Kevin, the same unit and was now part of his 'team'. "Hi Tyson, nope I'm made of sturdier stuff than that."

"My girl. Well go on in, it's lady's night tonight you'll be run off your feet before you know it. You know how you women get when you're out in packs." He flashed his killer smile and I couldn't help but grin. It had been a while since I'd grinned about anything.

I was surprised that a few people called me by name as I passed the bar to head to the back. I waved and kept going to the locker that I'd been assigned, feeling a little lighter about being here. Looked like I was getting another reprieve. Kevin wasn't here.

***

KEVIN

***

I told myself to stay away that it was too soon. But that shit didn't last. I was like a caged animal pacing back and forth in my place as the time for her shift to begin grew near. When I got sick of my own shit I gave in. I just wanted a look that's all. Fucking sap!

I pulled up to the restaurant an hour after she was supposed to arrive with my heart racing out of time. I ignored that shit. It's been a while since I let that particular organ rule me and especially where she was concerned no way in fucking hell was I going there. The only part of me involved here is my dick. And after I've pummeled her pussy with a few hard fucks I'm done. My heart could suck a dick.

I saw her as soon as I walked in the door. Like a fucking leashed dog my head snapped around in her direction. As if sensing my stare she turned and looked at me. It was then I noticed my boy Tyson in her space. Fuck that noise. I know Ty, I know how he works when he's moving in and he was showing all the signs.

I barely spared her a glance as I called him away. "Ty with me." He gave her a look over his shoulder and said some shit that made her blush before following me, and I wanted to break his fucking face. As soon as we were out of earshot I turned to him. One look at my face and his hands went up and he backed away.

"Whatever it is I didn't do it." That would be a first. Asshole is always up to some shit. "That thing you were just about to do. Not gonna happen." He looked back at her. "Hey, eyes on me. You even sniff the air she walks I'll break your fucking neck."

He grinned and relaxed. "And why would you wanna do that?"
"That's mine." He got serious on me and I tried to waylay his shit. "Leave it. Don't go hearing wedding bells and shit and tell the others to keep the fuck away from her." Bunch of fucking horn dogs.

"She's a step up Cap, good luck." He should know he's had enough of my leavings over the years. "How's Natalie?" He actually blushed and looked around. "Cap, why the fuck did you ever go there? She's a fucking pariah. I think she's into Pete this week." He shook his head and went back to work.

STARTING OVER

I'm always amazed at the human mind. I fucked Natalie one night while on a bender, probably reminiscing about this one, and ever since then she's been on my dick. When that didn't work, she got the bright idea to fuck all the guys in the crew as if that was somehow gonna endear her to me, or some shit. I know she didn't think the shit would make me jealous, it's been three years and I barely spare her a thought.

I headed back into the dining area looking for her. I had no doubt she'd be hiding. She wasn't stupid enough not to. I saw her at a table with Lucy, who I guess she was trailing and headed in that direction. I didn't let myself look too hard there'll be time enough for that later. "Excuse us." I took her arm and led her away from the table.

Chapter 7
JULIE
***

He practically dragged me into the back where it was dark and there was no one around because everyone was too busy on the floor. I didn't know if to run, scream or surrender. Of all the ways I'd imagined this going down this wasn't one of them.

My body was in free fall. My breath got stuck in my lungs, my hands were wet all of a sudden and my girly bits perked up and looked around. He had me crowded against the wall with his hands on either side of my head.

He looked down at me but I couldn't read his expression. It was blank. My heart was two beats away from jumping out of my chest, and my arm still burned where he'd touched me. It was like stepping back in time. The years just floated away and we were back there in his bed with him over me, in me...

"How long before your divorce is final?" I swallowed the saliva that had pooled in my mouth and croaked out an answer. "Three days." The first words I'd said to him in ten years and I sound like a hyperventilating rodent.
"I'll see you then."
"What...?" He was gone without another word, leaving me in a quandary. What does that mean? I stood like Bambi in the headlights for a second before my feet would move.

He'd aged well. There was a new hardness to him but that only added to the appeal and if I was going to react this way to him all the time maybe it was best I avoid him in the future. Easier said than done, I work for him. And that last statement. My heart beat so loud I heard it in my ears as I watched the door he'd disappeared through.

It took me a minute to compose myself. I closed my eyes and drew deep breaths as I tried to calm the wild throbbing between my thighs. I'd thought I was prepared for that first sight of him but I'd only been lying to myself. How could I have forgotten how hot he was, or how weak he made me in the knees?

I went back to work but could not for the life of me tell you half of what I did. I kept replaying his words in my head, trying to find the meaning behind them. I was afraid my body already knew. It's been a long time since I felt that dampness in my underwear. Geez he packed a punch.

After the number my ex had done on me I was sure I would be immune to all men from here on out. Who needed the headache? It had taken him, less than a minute to pull me back in the game. But what kind of game and who would be the winner?

"Hey, you feeling okay tonight? You seem a little preoccupied." Lucy looked at me with concern.

"Uh yeah, just worried about my kids." I felt awful for lying but what else was I going to say, that our boss had turned my life upside down with a few short words?

That led me to wondering if anyone knew. I'd seen Tyson look back at me while they were talking, and my face flushed at the thought that he knew about that night. The idea made me a little jumpy and I looked around to see if anyone else had seen him take me back there. I soon had my answer.

"You better watch your back. Natalie's been giving you the stink eye ever since the boss dragged you away from that table." Dammit, she'd seen that? I took a furtive look over my shoulder and found the other woman glaring at me from across the room.

I spent the rest of the night avoiding her and keeping track of Kevin who was still here but from what I could tell wasn't even looking in my direction. As if the stress of having to deal with the divorce becoming final wasn't enough, now I had his threat hanging over my head. What exactly did he plan to do?

That night on my way back to the motel I was very aware of a black truck following close behind me. I had no idea who it could be, and wasn't exactly scared until it followed me into the parking lot.

1

I sat in my car in cold fear not knowing what to do as every Discovery channel cop show I'd ever seen played out in my head. I held my breath when the driver side door opened and didn't really breathe any easier when I saw that it was him. He'd followed me home.

He tapped on my door and I opened it. "Let's go." I got out and followed him. How did he know which room was mine? The room was in darkness except for the TV. The kids were asleep on their bed and Tracy was on the ratty chair watching the tube.

"Uncle Kevin?" She flew up from the chair and into his arms. "Hey squirt how are you?" He hugged her like he meant it and I felt just a little bit jealous. Pathetic. I looked away when he started whispering to her and went to check on the kids. I protested when he tried to pay her but neither of them paid any attention to me.

"You didn't have to do that." I said after we'd said our goodbyes to Tracy and he'd told her like five times to be careful. He didn't bother answering and I was about to ask him what he was doing here when he spoke.

"Get your stuff together." He moved to the bed and picked my daughter up from the bed and not wanting to wake the kids I whispered. "What are you doing?" He walked by me and out the door with me following him. I stood in the door and watched with my mouth open as he opened his truck and placed her in the backseat before coming back to the room.

"I told you to pack." He went after Dylan next and I felt like I was in an episode of the twilight zone. Obviously he wasn't planning on killing me, why would he take the kids? But I had no answer for the madness that was taking place before my eyes.

I grabbed our stuff, which had never been unpacked since we've been living out of bags for almost two weeks. Just some odds and ends from the bathroom and on the floor. Pitiful. After ten years this was all I had to show for myself. Robert had destroyed most everything else once I got up the nerve to leave. At least that's what he'd said the night on the phone after I'd called him to tell him we weren't coming back.

That was months ago and had I not threatened to expose him to the media he would still be dragging out the divorce. As it was he was still making it hard for me to get alimony and child support. I couldn't help making comparisons between the two men in my head as I watched him move across the parking lot; not that I hadn't done it before. But even with his reserved animosity, I was willing to bet that Kevin Hunt was more than twice the man Robert ever was.

He was standing next to his truck with the door open when I walked out. He took the bags from my hands. "Is this it?"
"No I'll be back." I can't believe I'm doing this. I have no idea where he's taking us but here I am just following after him. Maybe I was one of those women who just caved when a man spoke.

Or maybe it was that look in his eye that warned me not to buck against him. Strangely enough his highhandedness didn't make me grit my teeth in frustration the way Robert's did. I didn't get the sense that he was trying to put the little woman down so he could feel bigger than he is. From what I remember he didn't need to.

He stayed by the truck with the kids while I went to get the rest of the bags. I went out with the last set of bags and he took those too and threw them in the back of his truck before closing the door. The kids miraculously stayed asleep throughout all this. "Follow me." He waited for me to get in and start up the car before doing the same.

I followed behind him twenty minutes outside the city limits. It was dark out and all I could make out were the quaint little houses with their postcard lawns and the prerequisite large oak in the front yard.

I didn't remember this part of town, but knew it was in a better place than the one we just left. Is this where he lived? My heart picked up speed at the thought and when he pulled into one of the driveways and the garage door went up I thought I would pass out.

"What are we doing here?" He put a finger to his lips for quiet as he took my son from the backseat. "Bring your daughter inside it's getting cold out here." I did as he said still no wiser to what was going on.

Inside the house didn't look very lived in. There was furniture and curtains at the windows but the place had that feel about it that said there was no life there and hadn't been for a while.

I followed him down the hallway to a bedroom where he placed Dylan on the bed and pulled the covers up over him. I went to put Tiana next to him but Kevin stopped me.

"No, her room's down the hall. Next to yours." I walked down the hallway on shaky legs and found the room. There was still a faint smell of paint in the air and I noticed for the first time that the sheets and covers were new. I put Tiana to bed and kissed her forehead before stepping back.

I didn't realize he'd followed me in until I bumped into his hard chest. Everything in me went on high alert and my skin tingled where we touched. When he lowered his head and his lips touched my ear I felt liquid rush from my body and pool between my shaky legs. "They should've been mine." With that he turned and left and I stood there in shock. What could he possibly mean?

Don't be an idiot Julie, you know exactly what he means and that tone leaves no question as to what he has in store for you. I swallowed hard and forced myself to leave the room behind him. Oh crap what's he gonna do to me? Did I really convince myself that he would forget? That he never thought of that night?

Somehow I had comforted myself over the years with that thought. It was only weeks after my honeymoon that I realized how selfish I had been. I never told him about my upcoming wedding for obvious reasons. But how could I explain that that one night with him was my one and only time at breaking the rules?

Would anything I say now mean anything to him? If I'd been the one in his position I would've had questions, questions that would've eaten away at me for the past ten years. Oh shit. Just get it over with Julie. At least this you know you deserve.

There was only one bedroom left and I walked there and stopped short in the doorway when I saw him there, taking off his shirt. What the hell? He turned and looked at me and my knees grew weak. "Come to bed it's late."
"Kevin..."

"Bed legs."

I stood there transfixed wondering if I'd drunk something more than the soda I'd had just before leaving the bar. Had someone slipped me something? That could be the only explanation for this out of world experience. I knew it wasn't a dream, because his body wasn't the one I remembered, the one I had seen in my dreams more than once. This one was harder, more defined, and he was covered in ink, tattoos.

I swallowed around the rapidly forming lump in my throat and looked back down the hall. "I'll just go sleep with…" I didn't get to finish since he took a few short strides to my side and pulled me into the room.

The next thing I knew he was tugging at my shirt and I was batting his hands away. "This is crazy. I'm not having sex with you." Liar, you can already feel him.
"Oh when I'm ready to fuck you you'll know. Tonight's not that night." I believed him, so why was I here?

"I need to be up in a few, the bathroom's through there. Go clean up and get to bed. I'll go lock up when I get back your ass better be in that bed." He left the room and I had no idea who he was. The Kevin I knew had been sweet, considerate. This guy was none of those things.

I wasn't sure what to do, wasn't sure about anything. I made my way to the bathroom and cleaned the makeup off my face before taking a quick shower. Back in the bedroom he was already in bed with the table lamp on.

I'd taken a sleep shirt in the bathroom with me and now felt naked as I made my way across the room to the other side of the bed. I wasn't ready for this, but the thing was I had no idea what this was.

I climbed into bed and stayed as close to the edge as possible without falling off. My heart went into overdrive when his hand came out and pulled me into his chest. "Sleep legs." He reached back and turned off the light before wrapping his arms around me again and settling down to sleep.

I remained stiff for a good ten minutes before his breathing changed and I knew that nothing more was to happen that night. Nonetheless I did not sleep for hours after until exhaustion finally forced my eyes closed.

Chapter 8
JULIE
***

In the morning he was gone from the bed and I could not believe that I'd actually rested. In fact it was the best night's sleep I'd had in a very long time. I looked around the room and strained my ears for any sound before getting out of bed and going to answer nature's call.

I tiptoed down the hallway and almost had a heart attack when I found first my daughter's and then my son's bed empty. I was about to go into full blown panic mode until I heard Dylan's giggle coming from the direction of the kitchen I'd barely made out in the dark last night.

Tying the robe I'd found hanging behind the bathroom door snuggly around my waist, I headed in the direction of the unfamiliar sound and came upon quite a sight. Kevin was at the stove with spatula in hand and on either side of him were my children. Tiana was standing on a chair to his left while Dylan stood to his right.

The three of them were so engrossed in the pancakes they were making that they did not hear my approach. "Good morning legs." How did he know I was there? He hadn't turned around and I hadn't made a sound. Did his body tingle the way mine did when he was around?

"Good morning." My kids turned and smiled at me and Dylan even looked happy for once. "Look mom, we're making pancakes. Uncle Kevin let me make a batman one. Come see." Who was this kid? Uncle Kevin?

"Coffee's over there legs pull up a chair this should be done soon." He still hadn't looked at me but concentrated on what he was doing. I got a cup and poured myself some coffee while trying to clear the cobwebs from my head.

If nothing else the kids seemed more alive than they had since moving to the motel. It was a little surprising though the ease with which they'd just taken to Kevin. Like me, Robert hadn't allowed the kids many friends or too much dealings with outsiders. The only people we'd spent any real time with in fact were his parents.

"Dylan open that drawer over there. You and your sister set the table please."

"Okay uncle Kevin." Tiana climbed down from the chair and she and her brother fought over who was going to put what on the table. A loud whistle rent the air and they both stopped mid quarrel.

"Too early. Dylan you're the oldest, and you're a guy. She's smaller and a girl. Be nice to your little sister. You two work it out." And like magic my two terrors compromised. Just what the hell had gone on in this house before I woke up?

The kids had changed out of their nightclothes I noticed and their faces were washed and teeth brushed. It was barely eight in the morning by my watch. I'd never been able to get them moving like this ever. Mornings were always a hassle.

I watched and listened as Kevin spoke to them not like little brats who were under foot, but like little people with working brains. It was a change from what they were used to and it was messed up that something as little as that meant so much.

The kids set the table, Dylan taking the time to explain what went where to his sister, and Kevin actually pitched in. I'd never seen this side of him but then again whenever I was in his presence in the past I was always too tongue tied and star struck to notice much of anything. Except for that one night...

"Have a seat legs." Shit, I was standing there daydreaming. I went to take the seat farthest away from the head of the table but he pulled out the chair to his right and with just a look from him I was moving back around the table to take the proffered chair.

Why wasn't I chafing at his take-charge attitude? I'd just gone through hell to get away from one overbearing ego maniac and here I was letting him boss me around. Maybe because when he did it my panties got wet, whereas when Robert did it, it only worked to set my teeth on edge.

There were pancakes, scrambled eggs, bacon and toast, which Tiana proudly boasted of having made all by her self. "Thanks guys this looks amazing." Kevin poured each of us juice and even cut Tiana's pancakes into bite-sized pieces, all the while keeping up a running conversation with both of them.

I felt like a stranger looking in from the outside of my life, as my son who'd been giving me nothing short of hell for the past few months suddenly became this font of information on everything from baseball teams to the best tackle for bass fishing.

I had no clue where he got all this from since his dad never took the time to teach him let alone spend the time to do those things with him. He did do a lot of reading though and played video games so maybe that's where he'd picked up all that stuff.

"Maybe this weekend we'll do some fishing, I have a nice pond on my property, it's full of fish." My son's eyes grew wide and it all but broke my heart the look of want and longing on his face. It was on the tip of my tongue to tell Kevin not to make promises to my kids that he did not intend to keep.

Their dad had been the master of the broken promise and I didn't want them falling back into that kind of bullshit. But I wasn't sure of this new Kevin and thought it best not to challenge him just yet. I wasn't afraid, which was surprising seeing the take-charge way he'd handled us last night. With Robert his kind of control came with fists and putdowns. So far Kevin wasn't sending up any red flags and after the last ten years I know what those look like.

Breakfast was a noisy affair, and I relaxed once it was clear the kids were having a good time. I tried to take it all in but my nerves were all over the place. The man had practically kidnapped us, taken me to his bed where he just held me all night and didn't even try to make a move. Now he was having breakfast with my kids and acting like it was same old same old.

"So, how did you guys sleep?" I decided to take the bull by the horns since neither of them was asking the obvious questions. "I like my bed, it's soft and uncle Kevin said we can get pink sheets with ponies next." Tiana stuffed a forkful of pancake in her mouth and grinned at her new friend.

Dylan was his usual reserved self. "It was fine mom. I like it better than the other place." He hadn't called me mom in days, not since we moved to the motel. In fact today was the first in a long time that we hadn't started the day with an argument and him screaming that he wanted his dad.

"I have to leave soon but I'll be back later to take you guys to get some stuff. I didn't see any toys..."
"They have toys." I said defensively. But his raised brow had me sitting back in my chair. "Yeah mom but we had to leave a lot of them behind. I didn't even get all my games."

I swallowed the piece of bacon in my mouth and reached for my coffee cup. It was going to be a long time before I could afford to buy any of the expensive games Robert used to buy him to keep him out of his hair.

"Not to worry squirt, we'll get you what you need." He got up from the table and took his dish to the sink. I felt the burn and looked up to see him staring at me. He might have been Mr. Congenial with the kids but that look did not bode well for me. The lump in my throat was too big for me to swallow.

"You kids behave yourselves and listen to your mom." His words were directed at the kids but his eyes never left mine. And with that he was gone. I waited for the fighting to start but surprise-surprise they got up from the table and placed their dishes in the sink.

"Can we go out and play? Uncle Kevin said there's a swing out back." They both rushed to the backdoor before I could consent. "Wait kids let me see what it looks like out there before you go." There I go being over protective again, but it was hard not to be.
I'd lived in fear everyday that Robert would turn his venom on one or both of them. It had made me hypersensitive I guess and I'd never been able to let them out of my sight or without trusted supervision.

Outside there was indeed a pretty spectacular swing set complete with slide and a sand pit. I checked it over to make sure it was okay and eyeballed the fence that surrounded the backyard. Everything looked safe enough and the kids were off and running once I gave them the okay.

I sipped my coffee and tried to make sense of my life and the last twelve hours or so. It didn't escape my notice that Kevin hadn't said too much to me this morning, and other than that look he'd given me I had no idea what was on his mind. I knew enough to know this wasn't his home. Sandy had mentioned where that was and I knew it was closer to my parents than this place was.

I guess he had done well for himself if he could afford a place out there. Last time I checked those homes went for half a mil and up. I'd tried not to ask too many questions because I didn't want to give away too much to my best friend, but maybe I should've.

The kids ran around until they were tired and we went in to get cleaned up. Not long after I heard the key in the door and tensed up. He came in with his arms filled with grocery sacks and the kids ran to meet him. Were they that starved for male attention that a complete stranger could exact that kind of reaction from them?

I followed the three of them with my eyes into the kitchen, which I could see from my place in the living room. The house was built in the open-air style with minimal walls and lots of sunlight from the windows that wrapped around. I watched him unpack the groceries as he kept up a running conversation with the kids.

I was able to study him now without being detected. He'd changed, a lot, but all for the better as far as I could tell. He was more built than I remembered, his handsome face more chiseled. There were tattoos on his arm and neck and I was pretty sure under the close fitting tee he was ripped as the saying goes.

"Come here Julia." He hadn't even lifted his head, how did he know I was watching him? I got up and went into the kitchen to join them. "Help us put this stuff away." He was still treating me like a fifth wheel but at least he hadn't started yelling yet. And there was still that promise-threat or whatever you want to call it.

I reached up to put a box of cereal in the cupboard and felt him at my back. "Two days." Just like that my heart picked up speed and other places south started to tingle. I still didn't know what he meant by the daily countdown, but I knew what my body wanted it to mean.

I finished doing what I was and acted like nothing out of the ordinary had happened. My kids were standing right there for Pete sake, and I was thinking of jumping into bed with him.

"Let's go." Huh? Go where? I was about to ask but the look he shot me said don't even think about it. The kids hooped and hollered as they made their way towards the door. I opened my mouth to say maybe I'll stay behind and clean up a little but he beat me to it.

He pointed a finger towards the door and that was enough to get me moving. I was so confused at my own behavior as, like an obedient little girl, I went out after the kids and got in his truck. I made sure the kids were belted in before settling back in my seat.

I watched him lock up before jogging down the steps to the truck and getting in. "You kids all buckled in?" He looked back at the kids who chorused 'yes uncle Kevin' together their little voices full of excitement. He threw me a look before pulling out and I fidgeted in my seat.

I studied him out the side of my eye and my breathing stalled for a second. His arms looked strong and masculine as he grabbed the wheel. I studied his fingers remembering the feel of them as they slid in and out of me and barely squelched a moan.

My eyes involuntarily went to his lap and...have mercy. I looked away quickly before I was caught ogling his package. My face heated up when he chose that moment to look at me again. I dropped my eyes in fear that he might see what I was thinking, feeling.

He drove to the little mall on the other side of town. By the time we pulled in I was ready to get as far away from him as possible. Being that close to him even for such a short space of time was almost more than I could bear. I pretended a great interest in fixing the kids' clothes so I could avoid his gaze before we headed to the toy store.

"Grab what you need."
"Kevin I don't think…"
"Quiet. I don't want you to think about anything but what I'm going to do to you in two days." With that he walked away following the kids down the aisles.

Chapter 9
JULIE
***

That night in bed I was a nervous wreck. My body was wound so tight my limbs were about to cramp. I heard the shower turn off and held my breath in anticipation. Squeezing my eyes shut I tried to even out my breathing as if I were already asleep. I've never felt so exposed in my life as I did lying there with the sheet pulled up to my chin.

When the bed depressed from his weight I rolled onto his side before I could straighten myself out. I tried moving back to my place but he hauled me back into his chest. My body immediately went up in flames and that throbbing between my thighs picked up speed.

My heart knocked against my ribcage as his big heavy hand rested on my hip, before moving up to hold me around the waist. When he pulled me back into his body I felt his hardness pushing into my ass through the sleep shirt I wore.

His hand felt warm and comforting as he spread it open on my tummy and I wanted to whimper at the rush of heat that went through me. I needed to rub my thighs together to ease the ache but if I moved he'd know I was awake and who knows where that would lead.

His length felt warm and heavy against my ass but he didn't seem to notice. What kind of man was he? Was he really not going to try anything? I found myself wanting him to just lift up the stupid shirt, remove my panties and just…Oh good grief.

I gritted my teeth and willed myself not to press back against him any harder. I was already wet and my ass of its own accord kept inching back against him trying to get his cock to rub against my slit right where I needed him. Tonight had been my last night of training. After the shopping expedition where he'd let the kids get anything their little hearts desired, he'd taken us to lunch. "I can make something for us at the house. It doesn't make sense; you just bought all those groceries…"

Again he stopped my flow of words with a look. Had he always done that? I don't recall. The affect was instantaneous and I found myself closing my lips and following his orders. He kept his hand in the small of my back as we walked to the restaurant behind my kids who were laughing and talking with each other as my son held his sister's hand.

In the restaurant he crowded me, even when we sat in a booth with eyes following our every move because of course he'd chosen a restaurant smack dab in the middle of my old stomping ground. I saw a few old familiar people, some of them with questioning looks on their faces, and it wasn't long before the whispers behind the hands started.

We shared a menu and he was the one who asked the kids what they wanted. He was so easy with them it was hard to believe he didn't have any of his own. The thought brought me up short. Since I'd avoided all talk of him since my return I really didn't know that much about him. Sandy hadn't mentioned anything but...

"You're very good with them. Do you have…?" I trailed off at the fire in his eyes when he looked at me. I'm going to choke on my own spit if I hang around him much longer. I swallowed around the lump in my throat and looked down feeling chastised.

Did he really mean for us not to say anything to each other for the next twenty-four hours? Apparently so since he turned back to the kids without answering. Maybe he thought it was none of my business, which was the case.

His arm came around my shoulders and I felt warm and tingly inside. I was sure to the many eyes on us right now we looked like the perfect little family out on a lunch date. If only they knew what a nervous wreck I was sitting there with my panties wet, squirming my ass around on the seat.

Things only got harder for me when his finger traced a pattern on my arm as we sat waiting for our orders to be brought out, while listening to the kids prattle on excitedly about their new toys.

I had goose bumps all over my body from his absentminded stroking and places south were coming awake. "I can smell you." Oh heavens. He whispered those incendiary words in my ear and just the touch of his lips against my sensitive skin had me twitching in my seat.

I grabbed my water and drank down half of it before my throat stopped feeling like it was on fire, but there was no getting rid of the heat in my cheeks or the hardness in my nipples. When I dared a look up at him, he was studying me. It was the look in his eyes, fierce, hungry, determined, that made me squeak. He looked at the kids to make sure they were preoccupied before imparting his last zinger.

"Don't be scared legs, you've taken my cock before remember?" He moved his hand and turned his attention to the kids leaving me with hot cheeks, wet panties and renewed apprehension in my chest.

Of course I remember. I remember that he was so huge he barely fit. I remember being sore for days after, even on my honeymoon. It was almost as if I could feel that fullness now, between my legs. I ached in a way I hadn't in a long time. It had taken me ages to get over that feeling of emptiness inside. No one had ever been able to fill it and I knew without a doubt that no one else ever will.

Why was this all coming back to me now? I thought I'd put it away long ago, buried it with everything else I'd had to give up so I didn't go crazy. To me it was just a fond memory that I use to take out and relive when things got to be too much in the real world. I didn't know if to be nervous, scared or excited at this turn of events; or if I should run for the hills.

I could feel the heat from his thigh where it barely brushed against mine, and it made me jumpy. My eyes followed his hands as he talked to the kids animatedly, those big strong work rough hands, long tapered fingers. I felt a shiver rush through me.

I remember the feel of them over my soft skin. The way his calluses had scraped over my hard nipples and what that had done to the heat between my legs. I must've made a sound because his eyes flew to mine just then.

The kids were talking to each other about the games he'd allowed them to bring in with them so had missed it. I saw something come into his eyes. Something dark and heated but just as quickly as it came it was gone.

He let his eyes travel down my body, landing on my chest before making their way lower and back to my eyes. With my luck there was no way he'd missed the way my nipples hardened under my shirt and bra, or the inconspicuous way I writhed on the seat.

The waitress came over with our meals and broke the spell but I could still feel the warmth from that look. I squirmed on the chair my mind in disarray. My nipples were hard and achy, while between my legs I grew wetter. I had no control over a body that had decided to come alive, to once again join the ranks of the living. I couldn't deny it any longer. I wanted to feel his hands on me. Just one more time to feel, what I had only ever experienced in his bed.

STARTING OVER

My skin burned and that place deep inside me that no one else had been able to reach since him, throbbed and ached. I was going out of my mind even as a little voice whispered that this is what I'd wanted all along. That he was the reason I'd come back with my tail between my legs. I might as well accept it, as I'd learned to accept long ago that I never should've left.

I was beginning to feel sorry for myself as I sat in silence, picking at my food, while the three of them chatted away like long lost friends. He was so easy with the kids, so open and honest. He handled them like what they were, the products of a broken home. His manner soft and easy going in direct contrast to the way he treated their mother.

I felt so lost sitting there as I finally realized that he didn't want me. Other than that 'two days' threat, and sleeping next to me the night before, there was no real contact between us. He hadn't even smiled at me, and when I do catch his eyes on me there's always a sense of danger in his look.

Funny, but the more he ignored me the more time I spent looking at him. It was almost as if I were starved for his attention. His scent, that clean manly outdoorsy type that makes women think of wild sex on a hot summer's day, teased my senses and made me wish...

He shifted in his seat and I made the mistake of letting my eyes fall to his lap. I had to swallow the drool that pooled in my mouth. His cock pressed against his zipper and my neck grew hot until that heat crept into my face. I closed my eyes against the sight and the memories that flooded my mind. Kevin leaning over me with his arms outstretched so he wouldn't crush me beneath his weight.

Kevin rubbing his cock, back and forth over my wet slit where his mouth had just been. And best of all Kevin sliding in and out of me so slowly, so sweetly that it had brought tears to my eyes. What kind of lover would he be now, ten years later? It was obvious he had grown, changed, in many ways.

STARTING OVER

Was he an even better lover now too? It was hard to imagine that he could be any better. But this hard man sitting next to me didn't look like he would do slow and sweet. He looked more like the type to leave a woman wilted and thoroughly fucked, sore. Yes and you Julie want him anyway you can.

My hands started to shake so hard I dropped my fork. They all turned to look at me, but only he knew what was wrong. His eyes went right to my nipples that were still pressed hard against my shirt through the soft material of my bra.

He'd given me that knowing look like he could see right into me. He'd carried on eating and talking to the kids while his hand had dropped to my thigh. For the rest of the meal he'd tormented me by running his fingers up and down my inner thigh through my jeans.

When his hand reached the top of my thigh he'd rubbed the backs of his fingers up and down in my crotch and it was all I could do not to whimper out loud as I sat there trying my best not to spread my legs open wider so I could feel more of him.

It was the longest damn lunch in creation and when it was over I walked out of there just knowing that everyone could hear the squish in my underwear as I walked by. He'd given me one of his patented looks that did nothing to ease the ache and I just knew that he could still read my body, even after all these years.

If that wasn't bad enough, after the sitter had shown up and I'd gone off to work, I was still twitchy. Kevin had dropped us off after lunch with a goodbye to the kids and just another smoldering look that I couldn't read for me. I couldn't tell if he wanted to fuck me or strangle me from the way he looked at me.

The restaurant was easier than the first two days, since I was getting the hang of it. I did notice that the men treated me a little different, almost with reverence. The teasing was still there but the tone had changed.

Tyson was more attentive too. I saw him having private talks with one or two bikers who'd been a bit too forceful in trying to get my attention. After that it was as if someone had put out a sign that said I was off limits. I knew something was up by the way Natalie stomped around and sulked, but no one had come right out and said anything to me. Whatever it was I knew Kevin had a hand in it.

By mid shift I was counting down the hours and feeling a bit grouchy because Kevin wasn't here. Each time the door opened I looked with heart racing expecting to see his handsome face coming through the door, only to be disappointed by someone else coming in.

I was still semi aroused from this afternoon and with no relief in sight I knew it was going to be a long night. It was as if my body was preparing itself for something. Those two days were almost up. It's all I've been able to think about all evening as I went from table to table serving drinks and food and avoiding the pawing hands of a few over zealous admirers.

I don't remember when I'd ever felt this rush of excitement that was almost like a high. Not even our one night together which had been unplanned had made me feel this breathless anxiety. Every nerve ending in my body hummed. Every other thought was of him.

Just as my last training shift came to an end I felt the hairs on my neck and arms stand on end and my body became heatedly flushed. I didn't have to look to know that he was finally here. My knees went weak and my hands shook. I had to put down the tray of empties before they all went crashing to the floor.

I watched from beneath lowered lids as he made the rounds. Talking to his security team, saying hello to some of the regulars. He looked in my direction until I lifted my head, but then he just disappeared down the hallway to the back where the offices are.

I felt deflated and embarrassed. Here I was pining for the sight of him and he could care less. I was so confused by then I didn't know which way was up. Why had he taken me and my kids to what I now knew was one of his rental homes? Why was he sleeping in my bed if he didn't want me?

I'd had a hard time convincing Sandy that nothing was going on, that he was only being kind for old time's sake but I don't think she believed me. It's weird, I could share the worse of my marriage with her, but somehow I couldn't bring myself to tell her that I'd slept with her brother years ago. The night before my wedding to be exact.

Chapter 10
KEVIN
***

What the fuck am I doing? The plan was to fuck her, get her out of my system and move the fuck on as easily as she had. Instead I'm playing dad to her kids and watching her whenever she was anywhere near. Shit was involuntary. I couldn't help it. And her fucking scent!

I'd stayed away after lunch and into the evening because I'd damn near mounted her in the restaurant when I smelt her heat. I sat there eating a bullshit sandwich, when what I really wanted to eat, was her. I wanted to bury my head between her wide spread thighs and sink my tongue into her hot cunt until I got all her cream.

That shit pissed me the fuck off. I didn't want to want her ass. I didn't need to want her to fuck her and throw her aside. But by the end of the night I missed her so much I'd given in and came here. I could feel her eyes on me and it took everything in me not to go to her and claim her for all the world to see. Before I made a complete fool of myself I headed for my office in back to calm the fuck down.

"Hello big brother, what brings you here?" Pain in the ass sauntered into my office as soon as I sat behind the desk. "I own the place." She just grinned at my surly attitude and came deeper into the room like I'd invited her.

"Is there something going on with you and Julie that I don't know about?"
"Like what? She's your friend why don't you ask her?" If she hadn't told her about us she must have her reasons. Shame most likely. For using me to get off the night before her marriage to her pansy ass fuck of a husband. Who the fuck deserts their wife and kids?

I sometimes wondered if she'd fucked me as a one off. You know, good girl taking a walk on the wild side with someone from the wrong side of the tracks. That shit fucked with my head the most. There was no other explanation for what she had done.

That whole night she'd never mentioned the fact that she was engaged and not for the first time I wondered why no one had mentioned it. I was sure they hadn't because I never would've gone there if they had. But she knew.

She'd slipped off her engagement ring and onto my cock with ease. Something I would never have believed the innocent girl I'd come to know over the years capable of. Just goes to show. At least she'd taught me a valuable lesson. After her I never gave any part of myself to another woman. I fucked when I needed to, no strings attached. When I climbed out of a woman's bed that was it. I didn't give a fuck what she had going on the next day.

Sandy puttered around my office for the next little while trying to wheedle information out of me. I knew once I moved my woman... the fuck? I knew once I moved Julia into one of my places she'd start asking questions. But this was between me, and the traitor. I didn't want any other casualties, no innocent bystanders getting caught in whatever net I choose to entrap her in.

When she'd asked me about letting her friend have one of the rentals I'd said there was nothing available. That's when I was still pissed at her, plus I thought her parents would let her stay with them. Finding out that she was staying in that rat hole had pissed me the fuck off and then I was pissed at myself for even caring.

1 | STARTING OVER
10

Once Sandy left I turned to the floor monitors and looked for her. She was a fast learner I'd give her that. More than one patron had sung her praises tonight, especially the men. They were more than happy to tell me how good of a job she was doing and what an asset she was going to be to the place, what with her uptown girl classiness.

The fuck does a biker bar need with that snooty shit? The only reason I agreed to give her the job was to keep her close until I was done with her. That had been the plan, so what the fuck was I doing here at the end of her shift sniffing around her? You know why you're here you dumb fuck. Because you can't stay away, because try as you might you will never convince yourself that that night meant nothing, that she means nothing. Fuck!

I threw a stapler or some shit across the room and felt better for all of two seconds. This was not the way this shit was supposed to go, but I'm nothing if not resilient. I'll go wherever this shit leads me as long as at the end of the day I get my pound of flesh.

With that thought in my head I felt more settled. There was no reason I couldn't change up the rules a bit. I was still in control. She won't get the jump on me this time around because I was ready. I'm going into this shit with my eyes wide open. Now that that's settled I turned back to the screen.

My eyes searched her out immediately and I found her easily enough. Even through machinery I had a built in homing device where she was concerned. She was standing at a table full of good ole boys that were laughing and eating her up, and my gut burned.

I was almost out of my seat by the time she walked away. I saw the way they looked at her ass in that short skirt and wanted to take her over my knee. What the fuck was she doing wearing that shit? It's the uniform you asshole. Shit!

1 STARTING OVER
1
2

The more I sat there the angrier I got, but now I couldn't figure who I was more pissed at, her or myself. I saw Tyson that fuck touch her shoulder and looked right up at the security camera with a grin like he knew I was watching. Asshole, I should break his fucking arm. When she threw her head back and laughed at whatever he said that was it for me.

I passed Sandy in the hallway on my way back to the floor and almost ran her over. "Hey what's your hurry?" I almost mowed her down, not even stopping to answer her. Little Miss. Social butterfly was at the bar taking back empties when I caught up with her.

"You're done for the night." She almost jumped out of her skin when I came up behind her and talked into her ear. "Oh, um, I still have one more table to..."

"Lucy can handle it." I waved Lucy over from where she was talking to some regulars. "She's done for the night."

"Okay boss." The poor girl looked confused but if she was looking to me for answers she was shit outta luck; I had none.

I frog marched her away from the bar and to the back where I knew the women kept their purses and jackets during shift. "What's the matter? Did I do something wrong?"
"Yeah, you did." Ten years ago. Of course I didn't say that. I pushed her back against the locker and wrapped my hand around her neck. "What were you laughing at with Ty?" Her eyes flew open and she tried pushing my hand away.

"What?" Like she didn't fucking know. "I saw you through the monitor." She swallowed hard and her eyes narrowed on mine. "Listen I don't know what you're talking about. I've already dealt with one controlling asshole, I'm not about to…"

Before she could finish that statement I had her body pressed against the metal with mine. "You about to compare me to the asshole who fucked you over, think again. Remember in this equation." I pointed between the two of us. "You're the one who fucked up. Now tell me what the fuck you were laughing about." That hand got tighter around her neck and I noticed the fire died in her eyes at the reminder of what she'd done.

STARTING OVER

"He was just saying something about one of the tables that's all." I was more than a little surprised when the knots in my gut unraveled themselves and that tightness in my chest eased. I held her eyes with mine wanting to kiss her so bad I could taste it, but not tonight. Not while she was still another man's wife.

"Get your shit, I'm following you home." I let her go and stepped back still in her space. My dick was hard enough to break brick and I'm fucked if I didn't smell her pussy heating up for me. She didn't move fast enough so I rubbed my cock into her middle and heard her harsh intake of breath.

"Move, unless you want me to fuck you right here." She jumped into action with a squeak and I walked outside to get some air. I passed Tyson on the way out the door and that jackass grinned at me.

"Evening Cap. Nice night out isn't it?" I growled at him and his grin just got wider. I was sure by now he'd pieced shit together and figured out that she was the girl I'd told him about that long ago night when I was drunk and she was heavy on my mind. It wasn't much of a stretch to figure out that Julie was Julia.

I refuse to call her by her nickname the way everyone else still does. She was no longer a Julie to me. Julie was a sweet innocent who'd looked at me with adoration and want. She thinks I'd missed all those mooning looks when she was younger. I hadn't, she was just too young back then.

Maybe if I'd told her to wait for me...No I won't do this shit to myself. She knew just what the fuck she was doing when she crawled into my bed and let me take her cherry. I slammed into my truck after giving Ty the finger. There was no sense giving him another warning because I know him. He won't quit until he had me making an ass of myself.

He was the one who told me that maybe she had a reason for doing what she did. That maybe she hadn't meant to deceive me. I knew why he thought that way. He was comparing her to the woman he'd lost years ago. The difference is his woman, was taken away by her mom when she was still too young to be his. She hadn't fucked him and disappeared the next morning with his seed still in her to go off and marry someone else.

STARTING OVER 116

She came out the door and saw me idling behind her car. My eyes followed her until she got in her car and started up and I pulled back to let her out. I followed her to the little rental wondering why the fuck I cared if she got home safe or not. I paid my niece and kissed her cheek goodbye while Julia thanked her and went to check on the kids.

Now I'm in the shower trying hard as fuck not to beat my meat. After being close to her at the bar my dick had stayed hard. All the way home behind her all I saw in my mind's eye was me spreading her open to take my cock.

I flicked off the water and wrapped a towel around my waist before heading into the bedroom. She was sitting up in bed with a look on her face. What the fuck was she expecting me to do to her?

I dropped the towel and pulled the covers back on my side and she jumped off the bed. "Get back in here it's time for bed."
"I'm not sleepy." She started edging away from the bed and towards the door. I knee walked to the middle of the bed and reached out and grabbed her arm pulling her down hard on the mattress.

"I said it was time to go to bed." Her eyes kept going to my dick that was bobbing just inches from my face. I gritted my teeth and watched her as she took in the size of my cock. She'd seen it that night of course. Seen it, felt it, touched it. She hadn't been able to take all of me. Her tight little virgin pussy had cut me off at about seven and a half inches. I still had another five to feed her and I planned on doing that shit as soon as fucking possible.

Now she was looking at my boy like she was trying to figure out how she'd ever taken all that thickness inside her. "Stop staring at my cock and listen this is very important." I waited for her eyes to reach mine. "When I tell you to do something, you do it, you don't question, ever." She opened her mouth to argue but I tugged her under the covers and hauled her into my arms spoon fashion.

"It's not a debate. Shut it down and go to sleep. One more thing." I grabbed her chin and turned her face to me. "If I see you flirting with Ty again or anyone else for that matter; I'ma beat your ass red." I dropped her chin none too gently and closed my eyes to get some sleep.

Chapter 11
JULIE
***

The man is a complete chameleon. I'd stayed awake most of the night listening to his soft breathing, my body tense, until I began to hurt. His hand was heavy around my waist as he held me like he was afraid I'd disappear in the night.

As I laid there I tried to make sense of the signals he was sending out. One minute he seemed angry and aloof and the next he was holding me as he slept. He'd hardly said ten words to me, and all of them seemed to be tinged with anger. He hadn't brought up that night and I wasn't fool enough to broach the subject. I was pretty sure though that his new treatment of me was all about that. My biggest worry was what form his retribution would take.

I woke up this morning with the sun on my face and the feel of something warm against my chest. It felt so safe and inviting that while between sleep and wake I'd cuddled into that warmth and smiled. Then reality came crashing down and my eyes flew open only to find him staring down at me.

I must've turned in the night and now instead of having my back to him I was plastered against his chest with my leg thrown over his thigh. I tried to jump back out of his arms but he held me close, his eyes still staring into mine.

His eyes dropped to my lips and I felt my nipples harden against his chest. His nose flared just before he pushed me away with a loud 'fuck' before getting off the bed. I pulled the sheet high under my chin and watched as he walked towards the bathroom naked and that thing between his thighs hard and angry looking. It had felt so warm and soft beneath my knee.

My heart beat wildly in my chest and my panties were once again soaked. Just how long had I been pressed up against him before coming awake? I can't do this much longer; something's got to give. One more night of this and I'm afraid I might climb him. That ache between my thighs was now an itch and I knew only too well who I wanted to scratch it. Oh hell!

I jumped out of bed and headed down the hallway to check on the kids not wanting to be there when he came out the shower. Finding them both still asleep I went into the kitchen to get the coffee started. I needed a little pick me up to clear the cobwebs from my brain.

I felt like everything was spinning out of control. I'd let him bring us here, take me into his bed and basically take over my life without a word of objection. Part of me wanted to fight him. I wanted to defy him the way I never did with my ex. I refuse to become the docile little woman again. But another part of me knew that I owed him. Plus I got the sense that if I ran now he'd only come after me this time. Might as well get it over with. As long as I didn't do anything as stupid as fall in love with him.

My heart pinched at the thought. Had I ever stopped loving him? I'd buried those feelings a long time ago when I had to accept that my life was with Robert. But now that that part of my life was over it seems the floodgates had opened up and all those old memories had come rushing through, taking me back in time. To a love that never stood a chance!

Chapter 12
KEVIN
***

I ran the water as cold as I could stand it before switching to hot. I did that a couple times until I got my body back under control. I refused to rub one out with thoughts of her in my head. That shit was for fantasies. She doesn't play any part in my fantasies, not since that night anyway.

I'd awakened a good few minutes before she did to find her pressed up against me. I'd been dreaming about her, again. Of course I was fucking her in the dream and it was the sweetest thing. I came to feeling happy with that dream warmth still wrapped around me only to find her in my arms with her leg thrown over mine.

My cock jumped and her scent teased my nose. It was all I could do not to turn her to her back and sink into her right then and there. She was making sexy noises in her sleep as she rubbed herself against me, and that smile…

I'd watched her face the whole time imagining that she was dreaming of me, and then her eyes flew open on mine. She tried pulling away and I drew her back in. And then I remembered that another man had had her. That someone else had woken up to her like that for the last ten years.

My dick didn't give a fuck. I could smell her pussy and he was trying to get to her. I saw the need in her and was so tempted to take her lips. Not like this. I pushed her away from me and jumped out of bed with my dick leading the way, pre-cum already leaking from my tip. I had to get away.

The kids were still asleep when I left the bedroom and found her in the kitchen getting ready to make breakfast. I had the strong urge to walk up behind her and wrap my arms around her waist, nibble on her neck. What the fuck is that domesticated shit about?

She still wore the shirt she'd slept in and her ass looked fine beneath the soft cotton as her hips swayed while she stirred the batter for whatever it is she was making. I poured myself a cup of coffee and sat at the table watching her.

1 STARTING OVER
2
4

I could see her body tense, hear her breathing change; still I didn't say anything to her. I pretty much wasn't planning to until after her divorce was final. I had it all planned out in my head. As soon as she was free I was going to make my move. But now instead of the one or two nights of hard fucking I'd had planned, I was upping the game.

Why not keep her as long as I wanted? I wasn't fucking anyone else at the moment and I was suddenly growing fond of the idea of having this one at my beck and call. I know how sweet this pussy was. And the way she'd rubbed herself against me I was sure she was ready. I wonder if she knew she'd called out my name just before she opened her eyes.

She shouldn't have done that shit. That had opened the door to a whole lot of possibilities. I didn't feel even an ounce of guilt for what I was thinking. As far as I'm concerned it's payback time. The fact that I was taking advantage of her situation didn't mean a damn thing. She'd started this shit and although it had taken ten years, it was more than past time to collect.

"Pack some stuff for you and the kids, I'm taking you to my house." She turned from the stove to look at me and I could see her trying to gauge my mood.

"Why are we going to your house?" I raised my brow at her and she did that swallowing shit again. "No questions remember?"

She turned back around and I went back to my coffee. I bit back the little kernel of conscience that tried to rear its head. There was no room for that shit here. I was going against everything I stood for. It's more my style to help a damsel in distress. I wanted to hurt this one, bad. At least when I was done she would know the fuck why. Unlike me who'd had to wait ten years for answers. Answers I still hadn't found but was sure I would get them out of her ass right after I empty my nuts in her the first time.

I wanted to make her suffer the same empty desolate feeling I had all those weeks and months that I questioned why she'd done what she did. It hadn't been easy living with the feeling of inadequacy. Before her, I never doubted myself about anything. I knew what I wanted and went after it, no reservations.

STARTING OVER

26

After the shit she pulled I went into a funk that had taken me damn near years to get out of and there were days when I still didn't think it was out of my system. Now I have her in my sights and I'll be fucked if I'm gonna let her get away again.

I'm not interested in any excuses or apologies. The time for that has come and gone a thousand times over. Now it's time for retribution and I couldn't have planned it better myself. I knew she was nervous as fuck as she pretended to ignore me. I wanted her more than a little bit nervous though. I want her jumping out of her skin at shadows, wondering what I'll do next.

I'm sure she knew what day today was. I'm sure she remembers the only words I said to her at the club that first night. As I sat there watching her ass move under her nightshirt, adjusting my cock that had no manners and no discerning qualities whatsofuckingever, I realized that I hadn't even allowed myself to really look at her.

These past few days I've been seeing the young girl that had climbed in and out of my bed that night. I had stubbornly not allowed myself to look, not while she was still another man's wife. In a few hours that shit will be dead and then I'll make her understand why she should never have come back here.

Chapter 13
JULIE
***

I can feel him boring holes in my back with his eyes as he sat there silently. My face burned and I was afraid to look back at him again. My hands shook as I rolled out the dough for the biscuits and formed the little balls that would bake into flaky goodness.

I had the gravy going and was browning the sausage. I wish the kids would wake up. Just when I need them here as a buffer they decide to sleep in. Figures. I never realized how uncomfortable silence could be. With Robert it was a blessing, with Kevin it left me on tenterhooks, not to mention what the feel of his eyes on my body did to my heart rate.

He was so silent, so still. Like a big cat getting ready to pounce on his prey. It made the situation that much more intense. I moved around the kitchen doing my best to ignore his presence but I might as well have tried to stop breathing. There was no ignoring Kevin Hunt. Instead I let my mind drift the way it has been more and more here of late.

I remembered the sweet blush of youth and that first crush. He'd always stood a head above everyone else in my eyes. Ever since the day my best friend introduced me to her older brother home from the war. I think we were fourteen or fifteen then.

I'd taken one look at his dark sexy looks and fell hard and fast. It was the most excruciating thing, I remember. Me, the awkward, gangly teenager, with braces and wild hair that I could never get to do what I want, and him, the ultimate bad boy that all the girls were after.

He'd been kind back then and I think I fell in love with him more. He didn't make me feel stupid though I was sure he had to know about my stupid girl's heart. How could he not? The way I used to moon over him whenever he was near. The way I'd follow him with my eyes whenever he walked into the room.

STARTING OVER

Unlike most crushes mine hadn't faded away and died. Each time I saw him I found something else to love about him. I loved the way he and his family were, with his little sister. Loved that he started sending me little gifts whenever he'd send something home for Sandy and his mom from whatever port he'd stopped in. It made me feel special, like I was part of the family. Like he was thinking about me. I still had every one of those souvenirs in one of the bags I'd brought with me.

No matter how much I'd told myself over the years that I needed to let go of the past, of him. I couldn't bring myself to part with the only thing I had left of him. And until a few short days ago the only thing I thought I ever would for the rest of my life.

Has it only been a few days? Have mercy, it feels like we've lived a lifetime already and yet nothing had really been said or done. The smell of cooking meat brought me back from my trip down memory lane. It was just as well; those memories had no place here now. I'd chuffed things up there I'm afraid and there was no going back to that time. To that girl who'd had stars in her eyes and hope in her heart. If he wasn't sitting back there watching me I think I might've cried.

I heard the kids moving around in their rooms before their little feet headed for the bathroom to get cleaned up. It wasn't long before they both came into the kitchen still rubbing sleep from their eyes. They both broke into wide grins at the sight of him and I watched as my little girl held up her arms to be picked up after greeting me good morning.

I held my breath waiting for him to rebuff her and noticed my son was watching too, his little body tense as if waiting for a blow. "Good morning princess and how did you sleep?" He picked her up as if he'd been doing it for years and then turned his attention to my son.

STARTING OVER

"Morning Dylan you look well rested; have a seat. I'll get you both some milk while your mom finishes up breakfast." He asked them about their night with his niece and seemed to listen attentively to their every word. I hadn't seen Dylan this animated in a long time. Not since the last time his dad had told him he was too busy to play catch with him.

I turned away swiftly so none of them would see the tears in my eyes and took the biscuits out of the oven. "Ooh mom you made biscuits and gravy, my favorite." My son exclaimed his eyes bright with excitement and greed. The boy do love him some biscuits now.

I looked at Kevin to see his reaction but he was busy seating Tiana in her own chair. Robert would've had a fit if I'd made something special for the kids and not him. And you need to stop comparing the two of them. It will only make you crazy and remind you of the wrong choice you made.

I puttered around as much as I could before it became obvious that I was stalling. I was still embarrassed about waking up sprawled all over him not to mention my own thoughts from a while ago. He watched me as though he could read my every thought and my face went up in flames. That's been happening a lot lately.

He looked at me, and then the seat closest to him and I hustled my butt into it. His face didn't look like he was in the mood for argument or debate. "Are we really gonna go fishing?" The hope in my son's voice was almost heartbreaking. I looked at Kevin from beneath my lashes and was already starting to format a ready excuse in my head for when he disappointed the boy.

"Of course, I said we would didn't I? As soon as we finish up here your mom will pack you guys up and you're coming to spend the weekend with me at my place."

STARTING OVER

"Yeaaaahhhhh." Both kids cheered and that sinking feeling in the pit of my stomach went away. "Thank you." I took the chance of looking at him as I spoke the words softly. All I got was a look that I could not read. Whatever it said went right to my vajeena. What a time to recall the silly name I used to call my girly bits.

I played around with the food on my plate still feeling the burn from that look across my cheek. Once again he entertained my kids and I was secretly grateful that he wasn't taking out whatever grievance he had against me on them.

After that announcement the kids tried to rush through their meal but once again Kevin surprised me. "Your mom put a lot of effort into making this especially for you. A gentleman would show his appreciation and take his time, not rush to get to the next thing. Take your time son the fish will still be there later." He smiled at Dylan to soften his small reprimand.

"Yes sir. Thanks mom, this is really good." I could see Dylan just eating up all that male attention and I wanted to grab him and his sister up and get the hell out of there because I knew that this time when the end came it would destroy all of us.

I dreaded breakfast coming to an end but while the kids were still eating and I hadn't done more than nibble at a few crusts on my plate, Kevin leaned over to me. "Go get ready." I cleared my throat and excused myself from the table before escaping down the hallway.

I stood in the middle of Tiana's room for a good second before going into action. Once the kids were squared away it was my turn and I found myself at a lost as to what I should take. What do you pack for a weekend with the man who stole your heart when you were too young to have him, and who now hates you?

I heard the low murmur of his voice in the kitchen and jumped into action. I threw some shorts and tees in a bag and made sure I had decent underwear and a presentable nightshirt. Thinking about bed brought to mind this morning and my vajeena acted up.

By the time he appeared in the doorway I was sitting on the side of the bed dressed and ready. I'll check on Tiana before we walk out the door but she's at that stage where she likes to dress herself and Dylan has been doing that for years. Without a word he took the bags from the floor and headed back out.

I heard him asking the kids if they were ready and then the door slammed. So much for making sure they were all put together. I couldn't put it off any longer so I stood and left the room. If I were feeling daring I would drag my feet, but until I knew for sure just what Kevin Hunt had in store for me I was playing it safe.

If I wasn't such a coward I would admit to a little bit of excitement at the way things were going. Instead of the instant blowup I'd almost expected, this long drawn out suspense had its own appeal. The possibilities were endless and just thinking about each and every one of them had me rubbing my legs together as I walked. Damn, I'm gonna run out of panties before long if I'm not careful.

All the way to his home the kids chattered away, asking him a million things at once and he took the time to answer them all. I sat in silence enjoying the old hometown, reliving some of the memories I had of the different places we drove through.

When he pulled onto a street just one over from my parents' place I thought for a second he'd changed his mind. I knew Sandy had said he'd bought a place closer to my parents but I somehow thought she meant the lower end. Just how much money do SEALs make anyway.

The driveway he pulled into led to a massive structure that was nothing less than superb. There were turrets and widow's peaks and a covered porch that wrapped around the whole red brick structure. The Grecian columns were white marble pillars and the grounds were immaculate.

I knew my mouth was hanging open but I couldn't help it. The kids flew out of the car once he released them from their seats and I was still trying to pick my tongue up off the ground. "This is awesome." Dylan gave a hoot and a yell before heading towards the back of the house where I could see the water of the pond. Some pond. It looked to be at least four acres long and about half that wide.

"Hey, don't you go near that water without me there." Kevin called after Dylan who came up short and trotted back to us with a grin. They both clung to his side as he took us into the house which was even more breath taking than the outside.

The foyer was white and gold with marble floors and a gigantic crystal chandelier with about a hundred tiers. I grabbed Tiana, as she was about to run ahead and was this close to telling him we couldn't stay there. I didn't even want to walk on the floor that looked like you could eat off of it. And I knew for a fact that at least one of my kids was gonna break something.

"Let 'er go she's fine." He actually took my hand off her shoulder where I was holding her hostage. Of course that was all she needed to go bounding towards the wall of French doors at the back of the house that led onto the deck. She looked back as if to say hurry up and he dropped the bags on the entry table and grinned as he went after her.

"I know what you see out there." He opened the door and this white mountain of fur bounded through the door. "Gunner, out." The dog gave him a baleful look before tucking his tail and heading back the way he came.

He wasn't down for long since he had two rambunctious kids who were all over him in a second. "He won't hurt them. Come let me show you where the kids will be staying." He grabbed the bags and headed up the stairs but I noticed he left mine behind.

That started my heart pounding and I almost tripped on the stairs. Once again the kids had their own room. Tiana's had its own private bathroom and there was another one across the hall from the room where Dylan will be staying. Once he put their bags on their beds he headed back downstairs and I followed.

Once down on the landing I looked out back to where the kids were still rough housing with the dog amid shrieks and laughter on the deck. He kept going to a set of double doors at the far end of the hall and opened them.

The room beyond was massive. The king sized sleigh bed took up a good portion of one wall but still there was more than enough room on either side. There was a couch and two Queen Anne chairs strategically placed and yet more seating in the sitting area off the bedroom. He didn't have to tell me that this was the master suite. And when he just dropped my bag on the floor next to the bed before turning and walking out again, I guess I knew where I would be sleeping.

Back out on the deck I got to see the complete beauty of the place. He must've had the pond dug because I grew up here and never saw anything like it. His house was bigger than my parents' and a damn sight much nicer than the one I shared with Robert and I wondered if the day would ever come when I would feel secure in asking him just how he was able to afford it.

I'm sure the restaurant was doing well, but this place would take beyond doing well. I felt a slight sadness leave me as I realized that this would never be mine. Not just the house but also the man who owned it. Even without what happened between us there was never any guarantee that we would've gone any farther back then.

I knew I'd missed my one chance and there was no hope for it. But this place, the beauty and serenity of it, made my romantic heart bleed. I could see us here, together. And the sound of his laughter as he played with my children made me wish for things that could never be.

I closed my eyes against the sharp pain and opened them only to find myself staring right into his. There'd been something there in his eyes at first that he shielded suddenly by lowering his lashes before turning away again. I had the sudden urge to cry.

142 STARTING OVER

Why couldn't he have become a bald potbellied slovenly pig? Then I could pat myself on the back and say 'well done you'. Instead it was only becoming more and more clearer to me, that I had ditched the prince to marry a frog. A big fat, disgusting womanizing, piece of shit toad.

I shook off the doldrums and tried to join in the fun. The kids had always wanted a dog but of course you know who, had said no. I find it strange that in the beginning of my marriage I couldn't put thoughts of Kevin out of my mind, couldn't stop comparing the two men, with my husband always coming up short. Now here I am doing the same but in reverse. There was nothing at all short or lacking about Mr. Hunt.

I ended up sitting around the pool with a book while he and the kids went down to the pond to fish. I'd heard him telling the kids that he'd take them out on the boat once he taught them how to swim. Unreal. It was as if some cosmic force was doing its best to strike home just what a screw up I was for leaving his bed ten years ago.

I should've ran away. At least told him what was going on and that I'd never wanted to marry anyone but him. But as a dutiful daughter I'd bowed to the dictates of my parents and lived to pay the price. I guess father doesn't always know best.

To be fair, until that night I didn't even think he had any interest in me so it was no one's fault really; except maybe my own. I could see their heads from where I sat and hear the whisper of their voices on the wind. I put the book down and closed my eyes thinking to just rest there for a minute on the comfortable lounge.

The sun on my face felt nice and so did the nice breeze coming off he water. There were birds and squirrels playing in the trees and the scent of flowers tickled my nose.

Chapter 14
KEVIN
***

She's still so fucking beautiful it hurts. Beauty can be deceiving. I stood over her for a good while just taking her in. I'd known the moment her eyes were off me. I'd felt it. And when that prickling sensation I get when she's watching me didn't return I looked back over the distance to see her laid back on the lounge fast asleep.

The kids were already growing tired from the sun plus they were excited to clean the fish that we'd caught. I left her sleeping and went back to where I'd left them at the little table I had set up to clean my catch.

She stayed on my mind the whole time the kids and I were talking as I scaled and gutted the fish. There were ewwwws from Tiana and cools from Dylan as they both made me chuckle. I like her kids. Once they came out of their shells they had proved to be well rounded well-adjusted little ones, with an underlying tinge of cautiousness that children should never have.

Each time they asked me something or to do something they seemed to hold their breath until I answered. Each answer would bring smiles and they'd draw a little closer until they were both up under me.

I chuckled to myself and as uncomfortable as it was to bone the fish with them there, no way was I going to send them away. Every once in a while I looked back over my shoulder to check on her, make sure she didn't burn in the sun with her fair skin. Then I'd snap the fuck out of it and remind myself I didn't give a shit. Yeah, that was working out real well.

"You guys go clean up we'll have your fish for dinner. You did good." They started to yell but I shushed them with a finger to my lips. "Don't wake your mother." My eyes were drawn to her again as I ushered them into the little guest bathroom off the kitchen.

Outside I went to stand over her again, my fingers itching to touch. I looked at my watch, still at least twelve hours to go but that time can't come soon enough, my dick's about to break the fuck off. It's been pushing against my zipper in one way or another since she came back.

STARTING OVER

I brushed a lock of hair back that blew onto her forehead and ran my finger down her cheek. The children's voices as they made their way back to the deck startled me out of my daze and I pulled it back. Damn you! She looked soft and innocent. The way she'd looked that night while I watched her sleep; when I let her sleep that is.

I knew now that those looks were deceiving. No innocent could've done what she did, not so effortlessly. I had to put it away because I had two eager beavers looking at me for their next game plan. "Okay, we can get into the pool and I can teach you how to swim, play basketball, read a book." I didn't offer video games because from what I'd seen they were both too addicted to those things as it is.

"Can you teach us how to swim now so next time we can go out on the boat?"
"Sure thing buddy." I clasped his shoulder and then his face fell.
"Oh wait, we don't have anything to wear in the pool." Poor kid looked like he'd lost his mutt.

"Not to worry kid I've got you covered." Yeah, uncle Kevin went out and got you everything for the weekend, because he plans on keeping you busy while he violates the fuck outta your mom.

I threw her one last look before heading inside with the two munchkins on my heels. Pretty soon they were both wearing their new swimming digs and were well prepared with arm floats and goggles.

She must've been tired off her ass because she slept through an hour of water splashing and squeals when one or the other of them stayed afloat or swam across the shallow end.

By the time I dragged them out which was a chore in itself because they both seemed to be part fish, it was time for lunch. I made soup and sandwiches and set them at the table before going to collect her. If she stayed out here much longer she'd burn for sure and I didn't want sunburn fucking up my plans. I have plans for every inch of that body.

I could've woken her up a thousand ways but the sap in me picked her up off the chair. She came awake cuddled into my chest. She jerked and almost fell out of my arms before I put her back on her feet.

"Oh I fell asleep I'm so sorry. They didn't give you any trouble did they?"
"The kids are fine. Lunch is ready." I walked away leaving her to follow. She was embarrassed as hell about leaving me alone with the kids but there was something else going on. None of your business Kevin! You're just gonna fuck, get her outta your system and move the fuck on.

As the evening wore on she grew more and more tense and by dinner she was damn near jumping at shadows. It could be all the silent looks I kept giving her. She always knew when I had eyes on her because she'd pink up and try to avoid looking, but always she'd turn those bright eyes of hers on mine.

I didn't try to hide what I was thinking from her, or what I was doing to her. I was on the hunt it was a game; like a lion stalking his prey before he pounced.
"Kids it's time to get ready for bed." If she had a problem with me directing her kids she kept it to herself, which was good.

It's just my nature to be in complete control all the time so it came naturally. Plus they seemed like they needed it and not for the first time I wondered what the hell kind of man she'd married that his kids seemed so starved for attention. If I had a son.... Nope not fucking going there. That shit is dead in the water.

She got up to help them get situated and I poured myself a drink as I looked out at the moonlight on the water. I think today was the first time since buying this house three years ago that it really felt like a home. I hated that she was the one who brought that here, that it wasn't some other woman who'd won my heart. "Fuck!"

That was the burn wasn't it? That she'd moved on and I was still here. I'd done a lot in my life since that night, but most of it was for my country. As for my private life, I'd concentrated on building up my finances and securing my future. If I were honest I'd admit that a lot of what I did was because of her. Because of what she'd made me feel after that night. I was never gonna let anyone so easily discard me like that again.

STARTING OVER

She came from money, married money. I knew her family lived right around the corner, knew that they thought themselves better than most. That's why my house was bigger, and paid for, and it was the best one for miles around. I wouldn't lie and say that that wasn't by design.

Though no one knew about our little indiscretion, I had a point to prove to myself, and tonight I was finally going to get the cherry on top. She came back into the room and looked around while rubbing her arms like she was cold. I watched her every move in the glass of the window and didn't move a muscle.

I was already strung tight as a bow. The closer it came time to take her the tenser I became, maybe she was feeling the heat of anticipation as well. She took a seat on the couch but sat on the very edge as if ready to bolt at the slightest provocation.

"I think I'll turn in early too it's been a long day." I watched her as she got to her feet. "You know where it is." I took a sip of my drink and clocked her as she left the room. I rolled my neck and loosened up my shoulders before adjusting my dick in my jeans.

I'd been even harder since dinner and knew that shit wasn't going down until tomorrow some time. I looked towards the pool thinking a nice swim my cool me the fuck down, but decided against it. I didn't want to cool my ardor, didn't want to put a leash on my boy. No, I want her to feel the full force of what she has coming.

I went around the house cleaning up behind the kids and making sure the house was secure. I switched on the TV in the den and turned it off two minutes later. Nothing was going to distract me from what was waiting for me in exactly…. I looked at my watch, one and a half hours.

I heard her in the shower and headed to my home office to get lost in paperwork. By the time I looked up I had twenty minutes 'til zero hour. I shut everything down and made my way calmly down the hallway to the bedroom.

She'd left a table lamp on low but it looked like she'd fallen asleep. She had the covers pulled to her chin and was as far away from the middle of the bed as she could be. I smirked as I headed into the en suite bath, pulling my shirt off over my head and dropping it to the floor before tackling my jeans.

1 STARTING OVER
5
2

I was tempted to go with cold water because in about ten minutes my balls were gonna change color, but I resisted. I didn't rush through my shower and only stroked my cock a couple times before pulling off. "Shit!" I flipped off the water and forced myself to take my time as I toweled myself off and brushed my teeth. All the shit I usually do at night before bed.

Five seconds left. My cock was already dripping pre-cum by the time I made it back across the room to my bed. She didn't even stir when I pulled the covers off of her or she was doing a very good impersonation of a possum. Works for me, I wasn't in the mood for any of her shit.

I'm sure she knew what all this had been leading up to. But just like a female I expected her to play games. It didn't matter, she owed me and nothing was going to stop me from getting inside her. I'd waited too long...

Chapter 15
JULIE
***

It was the most erotic dream. I haven't had dreams like this since the first few years of my marriage. I always woke up feeling so guilty, but the need was always stronger than my guilt. It felt so real, my body tingled in all the right places and in that deep state of sleep I relaxed and enjoyed.

His hands were on my body. I think I came a little when his strong hands tore off my underwear. The sound of the cotton tearing seemed loud even in my dream but I didn't care, my heart raced with anticipation. My breasts shook when he ripped my nightshirt down the middle and my tummy quivered with lust.

It was the groans that woke me, his and mine. My eyes flew open to see his dark visage leaning over me. It's as if he were waiting for just the moment I awakened, for as soon as my eyes found his he lifted my ass in his hands and brought me to his mouth. Maybe it's because I was in that half asleep daze, but I didn't push him away, I didn't want to.

I had known that this was coming, had tried to prepare myself for it even as I ignored the possibility. There was no denying it now. Not with his mouth clamped over my pussy doing the most amazing things to my body. If I'd been averse to him taking me my objections would've gone out the window. It had been too long since I'd felt this. Why shouldn't I take this for myself?

Had I been fully awake I would've remembered all the reasons why it wasn't such a good idea to let Kevin Hunt fuck me; but in that moment I couldn't think of a single one. I soon stopped thinking altogether when he swept his tongue over my clit before dipping it inside my pink walls and pulling out again. My body was on fire, and no longer under my control.

"Ohhhh." I couldn't hold back the cry even though I'd bitten into my lip hard enough to break the skin. His tongue felt too amazing and made a mockery of my restraint. I hadn't felt anything like it since the night he took my virginity. My body was already building towards climax and I felt giddy with need and lust.

I moved against his mouth in wanton heat as my fingers tugged at his hair. He licked from the bottom of my slit until my clit was in his mouth and he was nibbling on it, sending my pressure soaring. I felt something big about to crash down on me and came fully awake on the brink of the most massive orgasm of my life.

Ten years ago I was too green, too self conscious and though he'd brought me out of my shell and given me pleasure beyond belief, the intervening years had taught me to crave the kind of sex only he could give me. This is what I'd wanted, what I've regretted giving up. Now lightning had struck twice and I was going to feel him again. Oh hurry!

"Please..." My pleas fell on deaf ears. He just kept tormenting me with his tongue. I spread my legs wider and grabbed his hair tighter, no longer caring that I was acting like a sex-crazed bitch in heat. My hips kept lifting to his mouth as he fed on my clit while sliding two big work roughened fingers inside me. I could hear squishing sounds between my legs and my legs shook with another impending explosion. I screamed and everything went dark for a split second before coming into focus again.

He made growling animal noises as he tasted me, and my temperature went higher. In that moment I felt more desirable than I ever had in my life. I didn't need the words to tell me that he was enjoying my body. Without warning his tongue and fingers were gone and he was leaning over me.

My heart was beating me to death and that fear that was always present since seeing him again reared its head.

"Are you on the pill?" He had my legs spread open and his cock in his hand stroking. My mouth watered and I shook my head no. He ran his hand up and down my thigh until his thumb teased into the opening in my slit.

"When was the last time he had you?" My eyes flew to his at the harshness in his voice and I swallowed at the look he gave me.

"Just before Tiana was born." His eyes widened in surprise just before he slammed into me. Oh shit!

"Ohhh..." I'd forgotten how big he was and how much he filled me. It felt like he was tearing through tissue to get to the deepest part of me, but instead of pain the burning pleasure made me move harder beneath him. And then I came to my senses, sort of.

"Wait, you need a condom." He grabbed my face between his hands and the look in his eyes was almost frightening. "Fuck that, you owe me two kids and ten fucking years." When he pulled my hair my head went back and I felt him slide even deeper into me.

Now my heart raced for a different reason. What did he mean, what was he saying? I couldn't concentrate on anything but the immense pleasure that both scared and elated me. My walls were tight around him and it felt like I hadn't been made love to in forever. Robert's quick in and out was nothing like this. "I see you married a limp dick motherfucker." What was he talking about? I had a questioning look on my face.

"I can feel where he reached inside you, where you're having trouble taking the rest of me. I'd say at the five inch mark." He eased out and slammed back into me going deeper this time and I came.

My body bowed up off the bed and my mouth hung open in a silent scream. He was tearing me apart. Now I remembered why I couldn't take all of him that night even after the fifth and sixth time he'd turned to me. But this time I wasn't an inexperienced fearful young girl. I'm a woman, a woman who's desired this one man my whole life. For as long as this last, I want this, all of it, all of him.

***

KEVIN
***

"Did he make you cum?" I plowed into her hard and held still, pressing my pelvic bone into her clit. She's so fucking tight all I wanted to do was fuck and fuck hard. Her pussy grabbed at my cock and sucked me in deeper, her walls undulating around my meat as I started pounding into her again. I kept fucking into her and then holding still to enjoy the feel of her soft heat wrapped around me like a glove.

"Tell me." I fucking growled at her. She was trying to fuck herself on my cock since I'd stopped all movement. A hard slap on her hip had her behaving herself. She was on the verge of cumming, her eyes dilated skin flushed and breath choppy.

"I asked you a question. Did that pampered fuck ever make you cum?" She shook her head and her nails dug into my shoulders. I studied her eyes to see if she was lying to me and once getting the answer I sought, lowered my head to nip into her bottom lip. I don't know why her answer pleased me so much but it did. She'd already cum three times on my dick and twice in my mouth and I hadn't even started on her ass yet.

She moaned into my mouth and wrapped her legs high around my waist, her hands going to my ass to pull me into her. "You want this? Huh?" I pulled my cock back until only the fat head remained. "You fucked up." I plowed into her going deep with one stroke.

She cried out when my dick banged into her cervix knocking at the door to her womb.

I grabbed her hair tightly in my fists and pulled her head back so I could look into her eyes as I deep stroked her wet pussy. "Spread your legs. Wider." I tugged on her hair until she obeyed me. Her pussy felt just as good as I remembered, better. I didn't want the emotion that threatened to overtake me from being inside her again. I wanted to punish.

I bit into her neck leaving my mark as I forced my cock past the tight ring of her cervix and kissed her womb with my leaking cockhead. Her screams this time rang out around the room and crashed back down on my ears.

"Unless you want your kids to know we're fucking you're gonna have to keep it down." Damn I'd forgotten how noisy she is. That night I'd had to gag her when I wasn't feeding her my tongue. She whimpered and tried to calm her ass down. Lust shone bright in her eyes.

Her pussy leaked its juices all over my cock down to my balls. I pulled out of her womb not wanting to make her too sore, not yet. I shouldn't care if she hurt or not, but I wasn't mad enough to intentionally cause her internal damage. I can't spend the rest of the night destroying her cunt if I put her out of commission too soon. And I plan to stay in her until the sun comes up. My beast was off his fucking leash and her pussy was about to pay the price.

I pulled my cock loose from her hungry pussy and gave her my mouth again before rearing up and slamming back in hard. The bed knocked into the wall and something fell off one of the night tables. "Oh, so deep…hurts…" Her voice trailed off as she lifted her hips into my thrusts.

My hips slammed into hers hard knocking her back down on the bed as I fucked her harder than I've ever fucked anyone in my life. The old memories came flooding back. Anger, confusion, lust, they all converged at once and before I knew it I was fucking her into the mattress and chasing my first orgasm of the night.

I had a need to cum deep inside her. There was a wild madness nipping at my heels and everything I thought this night would mean went out the window. Instead of the vengeance that had fueled my hate and anger, there was something else growing inside of me.

As I fucked through her tight walls, gritting my teeth against the sharp pleasure that would make me shoot too soon, it became clear, like a flash of light going off inside my head. I grabbed her neck and pushed my tongue past her teeth. When she tried to capture my tongue I evaded, moving my lips to her ear. I held her head in place with that hand around her neck as I told her how it was going to be.

"You're going to give me everything I ask of you. Starting with the child I'm going to fuck into your womb tonight, and anything else I want. If you defy me, even once, I will make you suffer in ways you can't even imagine. Shut up!" She'd been opening her mouth to speak but there was nothing she had to say that I wanted to hear.

I pulled my head back and looked down at her. "Wrap your legs around me; tighter. Hold on." I lifted her ass in my hands, buried my face in her neck grabbing her skin between my teeth and fucked the living shit out of her. There was no point in quieting her. I womb fucked her making her pussy clench and release, the tight hold of her cervix sending shock waves through me from my head to my toes and back to my balls that were hard and full as fuck.

"Aww fuck, damn you." I pulled her up into my arms as my cock jerked and thumped against her walls, as my seed blasted out my sac almost painfully and covered her womb. For the barest of seconds I felt something approaching love before I killed that shit quick. No fucking way.

STARTING OVER

I didn't know she was out cold until her head went limp and fell over the arm I had wrapped around her back. She was still breathing so I knew she'd just fainted. I left my cock inside her riding out the orgasm. I took the time while she was out, when she couldn't see my weakness, to kiss her forehead gently. I could take this little bit for myself. I was strong enough not to fall for her bullshit again.

She came to still stretched on my cock, which had yet to go down. Her pussy came awake, ten seconds after her eyes opened. I schooled my features erasing all vestiges of softness. I doubt she even realized she was moving on my cock, or that those sexy little whimpers had started up in her throat again.

I eased out of her womb with a pop and leaned her back against the bed. I waited of her eyes to clear all the way. I saw the minute reality came back and she tensed. Good, stay afraid. I hadn't paid her tits any attention, now I will change that.

I ran my hands around the high mounds ignoring her hard nipples. Her body was hot, soft and firm beneath my palms. "Look at me." I tugged on her nipples making them stand up as her eyes came to mine. "Don't look away, if you do I won't let you cum this time. I want you to see and feel everything I do to you."

I took her nipple between my teeth and bit down just a little harder than was comfortable. My cock stretched out over her tummy from where I knelt between her thighs, leaking pre-cum onto her belly button. Her hot little pussy opened and closed as if seeking my heat and length to fill it.

I fed at her tits making them both red and sensitive with my teeth before soothing them with soft long licks of my tongue. One day, within the year, my son or daughter will suckle her here. "You want my cock again?" I teased her open slit with my cock, rubbing up and down to her clit while munching on her tits.

I slapped her ass again when she didn't answer. "Yes, please yes…" I loved that breathy out of breath whimper, I love even more the way her pussy reacts when I spank her ass. We'll have to revisit that soon. I ate at her tits, marking them as mine. The need to possess, to own completely rode me hard. I released her nipple when she came all over my cockhead that I'd lodged in her sucking pussy. Her eyes stayed on me just as I'd commanded.

I ran a finger from her pussy where our juices were leaking and around to the tight puckered hole of her ass. "Did you let that bastard fuck your ass?" She had been too shy to let me in her ass that night when I took her for the first time. The thought that she'd shared something with him that she'd refused me had jealousy burning like a hot spear in my chest.

I grabbed her hair hard and pulled her head back so I could see into her eyes as I loomed over her. "I asked you a fucking question. Did…he…fuck…your ass?" She shook her head and stared into my eyes. I pulled out of her pussy and pushed her knees back to meet her ears. Without warning I eased my cock into her ass.

She moved her hand between us to stop me and I snarled at her. "Leave it. I'm having your ass. I'm taking everything you didn't give me that night. Let's see you walk away in the morning." Fuck I hadn't meant to say that out loud. Her eyes widened and she looked like she'd finally got it. How the fuck could she not have known? I never pegged her for stupid.

"Kevin I'm sorry, I..."
"Not another fucking word." I wrapped my hand around her throat and slammed into her ass. Her mouth opened and she screamed loud enough to wake the dead. She tried pulling off my dick but I held her in place. I waited until the shock wore off before easing out and sliding back in again. "You're not bleeding you're fine."

On her back, legs spread and back, her pussy was wide open for me. I teased her clit with my thumb as I stroked in and out of her tight little ass. She was still wincing from the pain in her ass even though her pussy was pumping out juice at a steady rate. She's so fucking responsive it was hard to imagine that the asshole she'd married hadn't ever tapped into the passion inside her.

It was easy to see that she'd never let herself go like this. The surprise in her eyes each time she came especially when I pushed her past her limits was evidence of that. Like she had never been touched. Serves her fucking right.

I slammed her ass hard and she bucked. "Please Kevin…" I held her hips hard between my hands and held her on my cock.
"No take it, take my cock." A look down at her open pussy showed it to be red and enflamed. "Is your little pussy sore, huh?" I pushed three fingers in her cunt and went in search of her sweet spot.

She clamped down around the cock in her ass and the fingers in her pussy as I drove them into her relentlessly. "That's it, I'm all the way inside you." I played with her clit while easing out of her ass and strumming her G-spot. She fought to keep her eyes on mine as the pleasure clouded her vision.

"I'm going to fuck you until you hurt so bad I'll have to ice you down. Then as soon as your pussy feels better I'm gonna do it all over again and you're not going to say one fucking word." Her constant squeezing of my cock was more than I could take and it wasn't long before I was ready to cum again. "Cum." She threw her head back and screamed her release. She has the juiciest pussy I'd ever played in.

The tight clench of her ass around my cock took me over and that tingling in my balls started, my toes curled and I gritted my teeth to keep the growl from escaping.

I came in her ass and pulled out. Once I could breathe again I dragged her into the shower and started all over again.

After I cleaned her ass off my cock I pushed her to her knees in the shower and taught her how to take me into her throat. I didn't warn her that I was about to shoot in her mouth and when she tried pulling off I grabbed two fistfuls of her hair and fucked into her neck. She got her first taste of cum and I didn't pull out until I'd emptied every last drop from my nuts.

STARTING OVER

True to my word I had my dick in some part of her until the sun started creeping up on the horizon. "I now own all of you. Look at me." I was still buried inside her having just cum and knew she couldn't take anymore. I could've gone for one more round in her sweet pussy, but it was almost time for the kids to wake up, that' the only thing that saved her ass for now.

She was a mess, hair stuck to her face with sweat, love bites covering her neck and tits. I knew her pussy was on fire and I'd have to take care of her. My dick could do with some attention too since I'd fucked it raw. That's what happens when you fuck your woman five times in one night.

When she cried throughout that her pussy hurt I gave her my mouth but that was all the reprieve she got before I was fucking into her deep again. When I pulled out of her for the last time I slid down between her legs and opened her folds with my fingers. Her pussy was beat to shit. I hopped down off the bed and went to grab the ice bag I'd set up last night.

Back in the bed I put the ice over her pussy and she hissed and sighed. I masturbated her with the ice on her clit and she fucking ground her pussy into it trying to reach my hand with her cunt.

I flung the bag aside and brought her pussy to my mouth. I licked and sucked her cunt until her juices ran down my chin. "One last time and then I gotta go." I held her hips in my hands and slid into her sweet pussy. I hadn't said two words to her in hours other than grunts and moans and some kind of animal shit.

"I'm going to fuck you hard again." She tensed up as I slid into her tight folds. "Don't worry I'll get more ice for your pussy when I'm done." I fucked her into the bed with her legs on my shoulders and her hoarse cries ringing in my ears. My balls hurt from cumming so much but my cock just couldn't seem to quit. The harder I pounded into her, the closer I held her to me it still wasn't enough.

When my thrusts became too forceful and I knew I was hurting her I pulled out. She looked tired as fuck and her body was limp when I climbed up her chest and ran my cockhead across her lips.

"Open and suck me off." She opened her mouth and licked pre-cum from my tip. She ran her tongue around the sensitive head and hummed. I reached over to grab the ice bag and put it between her legs while fucking into her mouth.

She sighed around my cock and I moved the ice back and forth over her fucked up pussy. "Take me in your throat make me cum." I lifted her head by her hair and fucked harder into her mouth until her throat opened and accepted me.

I could see the outline of my cock in her neck while she gagged and choked on my shit. I looked down at her, so beautiful, and my anger rose again. She'd let some other man have her. Had given him children… I fucked into her neck not giving a fuck about her cries. My balls drew up to my body and I pulled out of her mouth and jerked cum all over her face and chest. She looked stunned but my raised brow reminded her that she was now mine to do with as I pleased.

I rolled off the bed and took in the destruction. My cock was raw and chafed and her body was covered in little black and blue marks where I'd marked her with my teeth. She wasn't looking so good and I felt a pang of sympathy. It didn't last long though; this was only the beginning.

"You won't be able to work today I'll have someone cover your shift." I walked into the shower leaving her rolling around on the bed with her hand over the ice bag between her thighs. I took a quick shower and dressed without saying a word even though I could feel her eyes following me around the room. I looked at her long enough to let her know I could feel them and then looked away as I put on my watch.

I got two tablets in the bathroom and a glass of water from the sink. "Take these, it should help with the pain." I didn't wait around to see her take them. Instead I left without saying goodbye. I heard her first sob as the bedroom door was closing.

Chapter 16
KEVIN
***

I started breakfast for the kids and got them up and dressed. I hung around long enough for her to make her way out of the bedroom after a shower to get the stink of sex off her, not to mention my jizz off her face. I watched her to make sure she wasn't any worse than I thought, before getting ready to say my goodbyes.

"You kids don't go near that pool or the pond without your mom you hear me?"
"Yes uncle Kevin." They were shoveling in eggs like they'd just done a double shift somewhere and were starving. I only had a cup of coffee standing against the counter watching her. I'm always watching her. And after last night I think that shit got worst.

I'd learned a few things though from our sexual marathon. Her ex was a small dick asshole, he didn't seem to know much more than the missionary position and he'd never gone down on her. Her eyes kept trailing me and her face was red as hell. I knew as sore as her pussy was she'd spread for me again.

I was tempted and my boy was already on the rise, but if I fucked her again she'd end up in the ER. From the way she sat gingerly on the chair I knew she was in for a rough day. At least she won't soon forget who and where she belonged. I rinsed my cup in the sink and ran my hand over the kids' heads before heading out the door. One last look over my shoulder showed her eyes still on me and I knew she was waiting for some kind of acknowledgement from me. I wasn't ready to play happy family with her yet, and maybe never.

***

JULIE
***

I feel like I've woken up in an alternate universe. My body was so sore that it hurt to walk. Between my thighs were still hot and tender and I hurried the kids into their new swimsuits that Kevin had washed the night before and headed for the pool. It was either that or sitting in the freezer with no drawers on. Still I craved his touch.

How was that even possible? The pain was real and only bearable because of the pills I'd taken. I couldn't even touch myself down there without hissing in pain, but still my body was primed as if waiting for something. That place he'd filled felt empty and my face heated more at the thought that if he came through that door right now and dragged me back to bed I'd have my legs spread faster than he could say the words.

I watched the kids splash and play while letting the cool water soothe me as I replayed the events of the night before. I can say one thing; Kevin Hunt had done more to my body in seven hours than Robert had in ten years. I could feel every inch of myself and even with the pain, it was the best feeling I've had in a long time.

I have no doubt Kevin thought he was punishing me for past sins, but the reality is, I felt more desirable than at any other time. I'd lost count of how many times he'd turned to me in the night. As soon as I'd tell myself he couldn't possibly go again I'd find myself being pounded into the mattress.

I had to cut off my thoughts when they made my body react and my own juices burned the rawness of my snatch. I wish I had some salve or something, but icing down and taking a couple pills every few hours would have to do.

Was it all out of his system now I wonder? Did he get his pound of flesh? As I asked myself that I remembered the look in his eyes when he'd said he now owned me. Why does that make me tingle all over? Shouldn't I be running hard in the opposite direction?

Robert had been possessive too, but somehow the two didn't feel the same. I never craved Robert, never looked forward to more of whatever he was dishing out. So yeah, Mr. Hunt may have meant to break me, though there were times last night that he touched me with such gentleness it made we weep.

STARTING OVER

He may be out for blood, but if this was the worse he could do then I say bring it on. Even with the pain that was feeling just a little better in the water, I wouldn't change a thing about what we shared last night. He didn't say anything about where we would go from here, unless that 'I now own you' was a declaration of future endeavors.

As I watched my children playing and laughing like kids, so carefree, I realized this was the first time in forever that I felt this...free. I had no idea what laid ahead but at least today the world didn't seem so bleak. I reached for my phone that I'd brought outside with me and saw I had a ton of missed calls from Sandy, and surprisingly one from Robert.

I closed the phone and rested my head back. I'll get back to Sandy later, my ex, not sure I wanted to. If not for the kids I would cut all ties with him, but he'd fought for visitation and won even though I'd proved that he didn't give a fig about his kids. It was just another way for him to exact control over me, and them.

Not today. I squashed all thoughts of him and went back to that warm place in my mind. My body heated up at the memories of his hands on me, the way he'd held me when he forgot that I was the enemy. I got lost in thoughts of how it would be if he truly loved me. What would that be like?

Chapter 17
KEVIN
***

Shit. I've been here for two hours and haven't got shit done. I couldn't get her and the night out of my head. I don't think last night had gone quite the way I'd planned. Instead of working her out of my system she seemed even more entrenched. The thought scared the fuck outta me. She's a runner; no way do I want to put that kind of trust in her.

I was out of my chair and headed for the exit in a flash. I hadn't even seen my sister when I came in and that's something I would've done in the past to get last night's numbers. Right now I couldn't think of anything else but how good it had felt being inside her. I glanced over at the passenger seat where I'd dropped the bag with the ointment I'd picked up at the pharmacy on my way in.

My dick got hard thinking about rubbing it in her pussy later to help soothe the pain so I could get back inside her again. I was surprised to find that I wasn't that upset at the fact that she was taking up so much space in my head. I felt a sense of...peace, happiness. Two emotions I'm not that familiar with.

As I drove I had to put shit in perspective. Last night had proved something else. I am a long way from being done with her. So what the fuck am I going to do to safeguard myself from her? How can I keep her with me? For as long as I want her of course! I wasn't planning any lifelong bullshit with her that's for sure. I don't think I could ever trust her. But that didn't stop me from wanting to have her beneath me again and again. Who knows, maybe I'll grow tired of her soon.

They were out on the deck when I came into the house. She wouldn't have heard me pulling into the garage from out here so had no idea I was there. That's how I was able to overhear her conversation with her ex.

"Robert you can't just call at the last minute and decide you want to see the kids, I need advanced notice. That wasn't part of the deal. No we won't be coming to you, you'll have to come to us. We can meet you halfway in a public place but that's as far as I'm willing to go." That's what she thinks. No fucking way. And what the fuck was that in her voice? I had a sneaky suspicion that I knew.

I waited for her to hang up to show myself. She almost jumped out of her skin when I walked up to the lounge where she was watching the kids play. She looked guilty as hell when I looked down at her. "Problem?" She shook her head and looked away.

"Who was on the phone?" She swallowed and twitched in her seat. "Robert." "What does he want?" She could tell me it's none of my business, but then I'd have to turn her over my knee for being stupid and she'd still have to tell me anyway.

"He wants to see the kids."
"We never talked about this. What kind of arrangement do you two have?"

"He has visitation every other weekend and two weeks in the summer, every other holiday." I thought of what she said as I watched the kids tossing a ball back and forth.

How deep into this shit did I really want to go? I have to think about this shit. Things were changing too fast and not in the way I'd planned or expected. Last night was supposed to make me immune to her, to release me from the hold she's had on me all these years. Instead I wanted to possess her in every way. The thought of her being anywhere near her ex didn't sit well but they shared kids. I'll withhold judgment but if what I was beginning to suspect was true, then I'd stop him there too.

It's then I realized I had a personal vendetta against this guy. In all these years I'd never let myself think about him. I'd focused all my hate and taste for vengeance against her. He wasn't real to me then. But after last night, realizing that she'd shared even half of that with him changed shit for me. "I don't want him anywhere near you." Fuck, there I go again saying shit out loud.

She looked up at me but I just walked away towards the kids. They were excited to see their new play toy but I had to disappoint them for a bit. "I'm going to put on a Disney movie for you guys to watch. I need to talk to your mom for a minute." I saw the fear and uncertainty come into their eyes, especially Dylan's and it made my gut hurt.

"Come here." I bent down and held my arms open for both of them. "Everything's okay, it's just some pesky adult stuff. Maybe we're planning a surprise for a little boy and girl." I kissed Tiana's little chubby cheek making her squeal and ruffled Dylan's hair. The look of relief in the kid's eyes didn't make me feel any better. If that fucker had done anything to her or these kids to put that look in their eyes I really would break his fucking neck.

"Inside legs, I'll meet you in our room." Her eyes flew to the kids and she turned back to me ready to argue. I lifted my brow at her and she buttoned it before heading into the house. I got the kids situated in the den with juice and snacks and headed back to the kitchen to pick up the bag with her pussy cream and went to find her in the bedroom.

She was sitting on the edge of the bed looking nervous as hell. "Take those off." I pointed to her shorts and saw the nervousness immediately. I also saw her nipples harden as she reached for her shorts and tugged them off. She wasn't wearing panties; probably to give her pussy some much needed air.

"Lay back and open your pussy." I was fucking with her now. I knew she was terrified of her kids catching her getting fucked and I had no intention on doing that shit, but there was no law that said I couldn't fuck with her. She turned red as fuck as she laid back to do my bidding.

I dropped the bag on the bed and stretched out between her legs. Her pussy was still red and swollen and her poor slit looked like I'd used it as a chew toy. I couldn't resist tasting her once. She hissed and lifted her hips when I licked into her pussy. I teased her for a little bit before pulling my tongue out of her. Of course my cock was full and leaking by then, but I had more control than a rutting teenager, I hope.

I opened the cream and squeezed some on my finger before slipping it inside her. I rubbed some on her cunt lips once I'd made sure her insides were liberally covered. "I'll put some more on you in a couple hours and you should be fine by tonight." That's about as long as I'm willing to go without being inside her.

"We're taking the kids to lunch get dressed. Not those shorts." She fumed a little but had the good sense not to say whatever she was thinking. Even though I suspected her ex had abused her in some way, I wasn't about to temper who I am so she wouldn't fear that I was the same. She'd have to learn that shit with time. "By the way, you don't go anywhere near that fucker without me knowing."

The reality is that with her unlike with any other woman of my acquaintance, I have the need to micro manage her ass. I don't know what the fuck that means other than the fact that what she wears is now solely in my hands. I don't want other men ogling my shit. "You should probably wear a skirt, it might be easier on your pussy."

I left her to get dressed and went to round up the kids. The four of us headed off to another restaurant and I kinda wondered at the fact that we were so close to her parents and she hadn't asked to go see them. In fact she hadn't mentioned them at all. I'll have to ask her about that later.

I got a kick out of the way the kids hung all over me, the way they tried to monopolize my time. Until now, spending time with them, I never knew how much I'd wanted this. No, I wanted this with her. I'd been lying to myself all this time. How could I admit that one night had meant so much? Only to have it snatched away in the morning?

I looked at her now as we were seated in the restaurant. Had I bred her last night? Was she even now carrying my seed? My dick sprang up and knocked against my zipper. How am I going to play this? There was a little voice inside my head with all the answers, only I wasn't sure I was ready to listen.

How can I marry someone who'd done what she did? On the other hand, I could never have a child out there without my name and protection. Which meant that that's exactly where we were headed. Maybe it's what I'd wanted ever since I'd learned that she was free. Sap!

I wasn't completely opposed to the idea of marriage. It was the best way to keep her under my control. The more I thought of it the better the idea sounded to me. As her husband I would have total and complete control over her. Just the thought made my balls fill and I had to give my boy a cursory pass with my hand to get him to settle. Perfect!

Everything was fine once I convinced myself that I would only be doing this as part of my revenge; that there was no emotional entanglement involved. She felt my eyes on her and looked up at me from her place next to me. I had my hand resting along the back of the booth behind her head, caging her in.

This need to constantly remind her she was mine only seemed to grow stronger with time. Before last night, before I'd had her, it was much easier to put another name on whatever the fuck was going on with me. But I got the feeling that the time would soon come when I'd have to admit some things to myself. That'd have to wait for another day.

Since the place I'd chosen was kid friendly I gave the kids some coins to play the little machine operated games that were set up to rob parents of their hard earned money. "Leave them." She was about to follow them but since the machines were in our direct view and literally ten feet away I saw no need. Her jumpiness when it came to the kids was another red flag. I'd noticed it when we went shopping a few days earlier. She damn near hyperventilated whenever they got too far away from her, even if she still has eyes on them.

"How are you feeling?" She seemed surprised by the question or the fact that I would even care. Good, can't have her believing that this was more than a fuck. I didn't want her knowing that she did mean more; that it was looking more and more like she'd never stopped.

"I'm okay." I just gave her a look as I reached for the basket of bread. "Is that true or are you just saying that?" I buttered a warm roll and placed it on her plate. She'd been staring at those damn rolls like they were the next best thing but she refused to reach for one. I'm sure she thought she was too 'fat' to eat bread or some clueless asshole had told her that shit. Only an insecure fuck would be afraid of his woman's curves.

She tore off a piece and chewed it slowly as if treasuring the taste. It's a damn roll for fuck sake. "It still stings a little but not like before." She looked down at her lap instead of up at me and as much as I'd wanted her cowed and on her fucking knees before me begging my forgiveness. I didn't like that shit one fuck.

"Look at me when you're talking to me." She turned her red face up to me. I had my eyes on the kids the whole time but I could still see her every move. "So, I don't know how this works, your divorce is final, now what?" She shrugged her shoulders. "Nothing I guess. I'm still waiting to hear from my lawyer about hidden assets but I have a contingency that says if any is found then alimony and child support will reflect that."

"You don't need his money." She looked at me questioningly but the kids were coming back to the table so I shook my head at her. "Later!" Yeah later! If I was going to take her on then I'd be damned if her asshole ex was gonna be giving her money. And as soon as I find out what the fuck had gone on in that marriage, if I don't like what I find, I will find a way to cut him out of her life completely.

192 STARTING OVER

    I hadn't done that deep search that I hadn't had time for a few weeks ago, but there was nothing stopping me now. I'd be stateside for the foreseeable future unless some asshole somewhere got hot fingers and his ass needed taking out. Hopefully the leaders of the world would take a fucking break from stirring up shit and I could focus on my own shit for a change.

    "Did you have fun?" I moved so the kids could be in the middle of us just as the waitress headed over with our lunch. I noticed that she'd eaten her roll and since all she'd ordered was a salad, buttered another one for us to share. She gave me a little smile that said way too much and I cursed under my breath.

    No doubt the asshole had insulted her weight at some point; she had all the signs. I wasn't planning on piggy backing on any of his shit so she'd have to get used to something else. I happen to like her curves. She hadn't changed that much in ten years, and what few pounds she'd gained were in all the right places. I especially liked holding her ass in my hands while I fucked into her nice and deep. Not suitable thought material for this venue.

I turned my attention to the kids as they went on and on about the games they'd played and the prizes they hadn't won. It was cute the way they vied for my attention. And a little heartbreaking the way they were starved for attention. Since that little niggling seed of doubt had been planted I find myself studying the three of them closely.

If there's one thing I'm good at it's reading people. It's a big part of my training and had helped me avoid some pretty sticky situations in the past. Another reason why the job she'd done on me had shaken me so hard. When a man's life and the lives he's sworn to protect depend on that particular ability, it's not easy when you've failed. I'd read her one way and she'd turned out to be something completely different. The problem is, after spending the last few days with her I'm even more confused.

194 STARTING OVER

She wasn't anywhere near the conniving bitch I'd believed her to be these past ten years, but I couldn't call her innocent either. She'd done the deed after all, for which there was no excuse. But I couldn't help but shake the idea there was something more, something I'd missed all these years or had overlooked because of my anger and hurt.

Whatever the case, I mean to get to the bottom of it sooner than later. I could brow beat my sister into telling me everything I know. But I wasn't ready to let anyone in on our little secret as yet. It was only a matter of time before everyone knew we were living together. Speaking of which…

"We're going to swing by the rental when we leave here and pack up the rest of your stuff. You're moving in with me." I ignored the look of surprise on her face and conned the kids with another swimming lesson to cut off any questions.

She must be wondering what the fuck had happened to her life but I wasn't planning on giving her the chance to fuck with me. I'm sure there'd come a time when she'd push back, but today was not that day. I had no intentions of giving her any say in this shit.

My dick had decided that he wanted to play with her for more than just a few days, but that didn't mean I had to go full asshole and open myself up to her brand of fuckery again. The sooner she realizes that this is not a fucking democracy the better. Giving her the idea that she had a say in anything I chose to do at this stage in the game was a big fucking no-no.

Chapter 18
JULIE
***

We went back to the rental property after lunch and once again I found myself in a matter of days, packing up. Most of our stuff had been shipped ahead and was still in storage, which I had to pay for in a few days before they take my stuff. Which reminds me, I need to go to work.

The sting between my thighs had downgraded to a slight throb that was more like a needy ache than actual pain and there was no reason why I couldn't work the floor. Which is what I told him as soon as we got back to his home.

He didn't say anything for the longest time and I thought he was going to say he wasn't going to hire me after all, in which case I'd have to hit the pavement again soon. "Didn't you go to college sweetheart?" We both stopped in shock at the endearment and his cheeks looked flushed right before he muttered what sounded like 'fuck' under his breath and left the room.

How could one little word, a word that people threw around so effortlessly that it had stopped meaning what it had originally stood for, cause such an uproar in my heart? There were butterflies in my stomach because of the way it had rolled off his tongue.

I was still sitting on the bed trying to make sense of it when he walked back in. "Well, didn't you?"
"Yes. But I don't..."
"And you want to work as a waitress in my restaurant."
"I never had any experience. Robert..." I cut myself off at the look that came over his face and barely restrained myself from jumping to the other side of the mattress.

"Don't call that motherfucker's name in my bed." I swallowed around the lump in my throat and nodded my agreement. "So you never worked in your field which is?"
"Finance and management." He studied me as if giving it some thought before nodding and leaving the room again.

1
9
8   STARTING OVER

    I didn't see him again until much later because by the time I came out of the room he was in his home office. The kids had finished putting their stuff away and were restless so I took them down to the pond. I didn't know the first thing about fishing but figured if my seven-year old son could do it so could I. I was wrong.

    It only took me twenty minutes to be bored out my skull but the kids seemed to really enjoy it so I sat on one of the Adirondack chairs he had set up down there and watched them. They alternated between playing with the dog and throwing their poles in the water. I had a slight fear that when this was all over, when Kevin had exacted his revenge and didn't want us anymore, that it would be hard to pick up the pieces.

    I was very proud and extremely happy when my boy caught a fish, and even more so when he helped his little sister catch one. The look of accomplishment on their little faces was too priceless. I panicked a little when Dylan made a mad dash towards the house to show Kevin his catch, but my calls for him to come back were ignored. I caught up to him on the deck just as Kevin was coming out the door.

"Look uncle Kevin look." He held up the tiny fish he'd caught with pride and I held my breath waiting. Kevin made out like it was the biggest first catch in creation and my boy was on cloud nine. Not to be outdone Tiana held up her even smaller fish and got the same treatment.

He made a big show of teaching them how to clean their own fish and I was left with three smelly people who somehow got it into their heads that it would be fun to chase me with fish guts. Gross. I would've gotten away too had I not been laughing so hard I tripped. Kevin had the strangest look on his face when I sobered up with my brats holding me down on the ground so he could get me.

The laughter died in my throat at the heat that came into his eyes. And when he leaned over to help me up I thought he was going to kiss me right there. Instead he released me as soon as I was standing again and he and the kids went into the house to prepare the fish for dinner. We'd all starve if that were all we were having so I followed them inside to see if I could help with dinner.

Kevin had taken care of it last night, but since it looked like we were a little more than day guests, I figured the least I could do was offer. "Should I defrost something for dinner?" He was back to those silent brooding stares of his. "Sure!"

"Geez, calm the enthusiasm." I mumbled the words under my breath but not well enough it seems. "Excuse me? Something to say?" He came up behind me while the kids were preoccupied mixing the cornmeal and seasoning mix he'd poured in a bowl to bread the fish.

"Oh, no, nothing." He cornered me against the sink and my panties got wet. I knew from the way his nostrils flared that he hadn't missed it. How does he do that? "Thought so. Talking back is grounds for punishment; keep that in mind." Why did the word punishment sound so damn sexy coming from his lips? I decided to pull the tiger's tail. "What sort of punishment?" He subjected me to another one of those stares only this time it was followed by an up and down eye fuck. "You don't want to know."

That throb became a full-blown pulsing ache and I had to grab the sink behind me to stay on my feet. I moved towards the freezer and opened the door taking way longer than necessary to find something for us for dinner because I needed the icy cool air to calm me down.

***

KEVIN

***

I'd heard them outside and moved to the window to look outside at them. That feeling of rightness overcame me again and I wondered if I were setting myself up for a fall. I'd been in the middle of rearranging some things to give her a job more suited to her degree. There wasn't an opening at the restaurant but I made one. I'm sure Sandy would approve.

I was sitting there asking myself if I was moving too fast and better yet if I was opening myself up to disappointment when I heard them down by the water. I was going to leave them alone to have some time together but then I saw my boy catch his first fish. My boy!

I left the room heading down to them since I knew what a big deal that was for a little boy, only to meet him coming to share his success with me. How could I not fall in love with these kids? They looked at me like I hung the moon. Yeah, but what happens when she fucks up again? You sure you want to get this attached?

I pushed the question aside because it was moot. After I marry her she won't have a choice but to stay put, I'd make sure of it. Then the three of them were rolling around on the grass and their laughter was like balm to my soul. A week ago you couldn't have convinced me that I would be willing to take on another man's kids, now here I am.

We moved around the kitchen in relative silence the only sound the children's voices, but you could cut the tension with a knife. That low hum in my blood that was a constant whenever she was near was buzzing away and I started looking at the clock. Still a long way 'til bedtime.

Dinner was noisier than the night before and I realized the kids were getting more comfortable here, they felt safe enough to be kids even though I had to give their mother a warning look when she continually tried to shush them.

After dinner and their food had settled I took them outside to play with the mutt. I had two reasons for this, one it was fun and two it would tire them out enough so that when they went to bed later I was sure of no interruptions.

Tiana came over and climbed into my lap when she'd tired herself out, putting her little head on my shoulder and I fell all the way in love. Geez, like mother like daughter. What the fuck? I wrapped both arms around her and buried my nose in her baby smelling hair. So tiny, so trusting. Why hadn't she been loved? The question bothered me.

I helped get the kids ready for bed. It was my first time overseeing bath time since my nieces and nephews were little, which had been a while. Dylan was trying way too hard to be an adult, to show me how self-reliant he was. As if he were afraid that I would disapprove if he made the smallest mistake.

Once they'd been put down for the night I followed her into our room. She headed right through to the bathroom and I was right on her ass. She jumped a foot in the air when I moved up behind her and tugged her shorts down her legs. Once she was settled I moved to her top and stripped her until she was standing before me naked.

I placed her in front of the his and her sinks and unzipped my jeans. I passed my hand between her thighs before nosing my dick around her slit until I found her fuck hole. One hard shove and I was balls deep inside her. I moved her hair out of the way and buried my nose in her neck

I wanted to take her like this with the smell of the day on her. Sun, and laughter. Her pussy felt so good I had to hold still to enjoy the feel of all that tightness around me, hugging me, squeezing me, trying to milk me. "Fuck you're so tight baby." What the fuck am I doing? Enough with the endearments.

I soon forgot about that slip of the tongue when she pushed her ass back into my thrusts. I leaned into her and covered her hands that rested on the counter with mine. When I bit into her neck to leave my mark her pussy creamed all over my dick, making it easier to fuck her tight as fuck pussy.

"Kevin, oh, oh, oh." Each oh had been followed, by a pounding thrust into her depths. When she went up on her toes I wrapped an arm around her middle and fucked into her hard. "Cum for me."

I dropped my hand to her clit and squeezed it between two fingers while sliding in and out of her, knocking into cervix until that little opening widened just enough to let my cockhead in. That's all it took for me to start hosing down her insides with cum while her juices ran down my balls onto my thighs.

I didn't let her come down before leading her into the shower and setting the water temp while shielding her body with mine until it was just right. She stood still as if not knowing what to do and it was obvious she didn't have much experience bathing with a man. Better not remind myself that there had been a man in her life.

I never knew I was the jealous type. I always thought it was one of the weaker emotions. To find myself consumed by that shit was not exactly welcomed. I soaped up the cloth and started to wash her body. I spent a lot of time on her pussy, not saying a word other than turn around when I was ready to wash her back.

I rinsed her off and was surprised when she took the cloth and returned the favor. I watched her under hooded lids and tried not to laugh at her red face and the way she bit her lip as she ran the cloth over my chest. When she got to my dick she swallowed hard and looked up at me. I raised my brow and she ran the cloth over my cock, which was now back to its full twelve and a half-inch hardness.

I stopped her hand and took the cloth from her, dropping it to the floor of the shower. I put her warm wet hand back on my cock and stroked once, showing her what I wanted from her. She got the hang of it and pretty soon she had me close. I pushed her back against the wall and took her mouth.

I sunk into her feeding her my tongue as her hand moved on my cock faster, harder. I pulled out of her hand when I was at blast off and got to my knees. I pulled one of her legs over my shoulder and opened her up for my tongue.

I ran my tongue through her slit and nibbled on her clit until her fingers snagged in my hair as she tried to pull me harder into her pussy. I lapped up her juices from around the fat pussy lips before diving back in and fucking her on my tongue.

I slid a long finger into her ass going slow while tongue fucking her sweet snatch, getting my fill. She came loud and hard and while her mouth was still open on the end of that scream I got to my feet and slammed my cock into her.

STARTING OVER

Her leg had moved down from my shoulder to the crook of my arm keeping her open for my wild thrusts into her body. Her back hit the wall each time our hips slapped together and we both looked down at where my cock was plowing into her pink gash.

"Fuck, so good." I couldn't hold back the words and no longer gave a fuck what she thought. "You ever fucking leave me again I'll kill you." Fuck me; trots of the mouth. I grabbed her behind the neck and covered her mouth with mine again sucking her tongue into my mouth while her pussy clamped down on my cock hard enough to hurt.

"Fuck, let go baby." She wrapped both legs and arms around me and held me tighter as she ground her pussy down harder on my cock. I held her up by her ass and pounded into her hard. Since I'd already shot off in her it was going to be a while before I came again, this was all for her. I moved a hand between us and found her clit and that was enough to send her flying.

I pulled her off my cock as soon as the aftershocks subsided and put her on her knees under the water spray. "Push your ass higher." She spread her legs and cocked her ass. I opened her pussy with my thumbs and rubbed the ridge of my cock all around her hole teasing the shit out of her.

"Please Kevin, I can't stand it." I smacked her ass hard and she squealed, looking over her shoulder at me in surprise. "You trying to tell me what to do with my pussy?" I tip fucked her before pulling out and going after her clit. Pussy juice leaked from her pussy in a constant flow.

She had the prettiest cunt I'd ever seen. Pink, soft, lush. I licked her pussy deep from behind until her ass shook and her sweet nectar exploded on my tongue. She grunted and fucked herself back on my tongue before I pulled it out of her and eased my cock teasingly slow into her hungry pussy.

"Ohhhhh...." We both groaned out loud as I sliced through her silky folds. I took my time stroking in and out of her with a reach around to give her clit some play. She moved her ass faster back and forth and round and round trying to get me to speed up but I was in the mood to play.

I teased her ass with my fingers, fucking them into her in time with my dick strokes in her pussy. Her head shook from side to side as she worked her pussy on my cock and came. Pulling my fingers out of her ass I wrapped both arms around her middle and pressed my chest into her back as I fast pumped her pussy hard and deep.

Her body stiffened, head fell back against my shoulder, and her mouth opened on a silent scream. It was a sight to behold and I watched her in something approaching awe as the orgasm ripped through her. I covered her mouth with my hand to muffle the ear splitting scream she released as she tried to rip my cock off at the root.

"Fuck, do that again." I hit her with the same fast pumping action but this time I fed her my tongue so I could swallow her screams. She did it again, it took five minutes tops for her body to become tight as a bow and she locked my cock off. I pulled back almost leaving her and slammed back in, going past her cervix and into her womb.

That was too much for her and she almost shook herself off my dick in the most spectacular climax I'd ever seen. How could anyone ever let her go? She dragged more out of me now than she had ten years ago. No way was I going to let her get away from me again. I'd do everything in my power to keep her with me. It doesn't matter that I don't trust her. This was enough.

We took another quick shower and then I dried us both off before picking her tired ass up and taking her to bed. I guess after ten or twenty orgasms she had no strength left. My dick was still hard and after last night I was thinking I'll give her little pussy a break. She had other ideas.

It was the first time she'd made the first move but she seemed to be caught up in the madness. She pushed me to my back and then remembered to be shy. She looked at me uncertainly and I ran my hand over her hair and pulled her down for a kiss. "It's okay."

It was all she needed to hear before making her way down my body and settling between my legs. She studied my cock like it was a foreign object, like she'd never taken the time to study one before. I clenched my fists and forced myself to let her do her thing though it damn near killed me

She finally took my cock in hand and looked at if from all angles before becoming fascinated with the pre-cum that had gathered at the tip of my swollen cock. "Legs you gotta do something or I'm taking over." She startled at my voice like she was surprised I was still here, so caught up in studying my dick.

She stuck her tongue out and with eyes locked on mine dipped it into my cock slit. "Merciful fuck!" I'd never seen anything so sexy in my fucking life. Getting the sense that I liked it, she did it again and again before sucking just the head of my cock into her mouth and teasing me with her tongue.

"Where the fuck did you learn to do that?" The undeniable anger in my voice scared her and I had to brush my fingers down her cheek to soften the tone. "Tell me." Her face turned pink and she let my cockhead pop out of her mouth. "It's like what you showed me last night." I smiled and dropped my head back on the pillow. A hand in her hair told her I was ready for her to carry the fuck on with the best fucking knob job I'd ever had. Then again I might be bias.

She went back to happy playtime and my balls were about to revolt. She found herself a new rhythm, suck my cockhead, then drop her mouth down my rod until her throat caressed my cock and back again. My shaft which usually hang a curve was standing upright and hard as he'd ever been.

"Pull off and ride me. I want to cum inside you." I helped her straddle me and pressed her hips down until she took me in. Her pussy was hot, soft and wet. She made an 'umph' sound when I bottomed out inside her and planted her hands in my chest.

I took both tits in my hands and played with her while she rode my cock. Each time I teased the door to her cervix she made a little yip sound that was too cute. I left her tits and grabbed her ass when my nuts started to harden. Pulling her down close, I bit into her nipple, drove a finger past her tight sphincter and slammed her down on my cock. Triple whammy.

She ground her clit into my pelvis hard as she threw her ass around in circles and came all over my shit. For a second there I thought she'd peed but it was just her juices. "You done?" She nodded her head weakly against my chest and I threw her to her back and pounded my seed deep inside her. When I finally off loaded in her we were both done.

I couldn't let her go so she ended up wrapped up tight in my arms with my leg thrown over her hip and my cock at her ass. And that's how we were when I woke her in the dead of night to take her from behind and again when we woke with the sun to do it all again.

Chapter 19
KEVIN
***

"Tracy is coming over to babysit this evening. We're gonna have to figure something out because I don't want the kids alone at night, we might have to change up your hours. One of us has to be here with them at all times and since it's better for me to be there in the evening when it's busiest, you get mornings."

I buttered her last piece of toast and put it on her plate. "What do you two want to do today?" She'd made breakfast and I'm guessing a night of hard fucking had given her the munchies because it was quite a spread. Eggs, toast, turkey bacon, beef sausage, home fries and fresh orange juice. I smirked at her and she knew just what I was thinking because she'd blushed prettily.

"Uncle Kevin is there a park?"

"There sure is. That's what you want to do squirt?" Dylan nodded his head and dug into his bacon like a champ. "Oh, I think I made too much food." She just figured that shit? "I thought we were expecting company. Like maybe a battalion." She kicked me under the table and laughed. It was such a domesticated thing to do it stopped us both in our tracks. I confused her farther by pulling her to me by the back of her head and kissing her.

Shit, I forgot the kids. By the time I let her up for air they were both staring at us wide mouthed. Dylan looked from me to her and back and then lowered his head with a slight flush on his cheeks. Tiana with all the innocence of youth bust my shit wide open. "Are you and mommy getting married?"

"Yes!" Three sets of eyes looked at me with two separate emotions. One was shock and the other was cautious hope. Dylan picked his head up and looked at me like he was studying the shit outta me. Good for you son. "Come on Dylan, let's go feed the mutt." I filled the dog's bowl with breakfast food and we headed out back.

Once I fed the dog we walked down to the pond. "How do you feel about me and your mom Dylan?" He shrugged his shoulders and kicked at a rock. "You know, if you don't tell me, I won't know and then we'll never be able to work anything out." He looked up at me and back to the ground but still said nothing.

"Do you think you could be happy living here?" I collected some pebbles to toss across the water and smiled secretly when he did the same. He watched my hand after a few failed tries and tried to mimic me. "Hey that was good son. It went farther than mine look at that." He seemed shocked that I was happy he beat me and I got that fucked up feeling in the pit of my gut and crawling up the back of my fucking neck.

"If we live here forever can we still do stuff together?"
"All the time." I didn't make a big deal out of it because it was obvious the question embarrassed him. He threw a couple more stones, deep in thought before he zinged me. "Do you really like my mom?"
"I've liked your mom for a long time son." With a sigh that was way too old for his years he looked over at me and said. "Okay we'll try it."

"Thanks." I clapped his shoulder and we headed back to the house where the two princesses were cleaning up.

Her eyes flew to her son and then to me. "You okay?"

"Yeah." Dylan gave her a little smile and once again Tiana put the shit on the table and didn't give a fuck. "Are you going to be my new daddy? Cause the old one went away. He was mean." Legs and Dylan tensed up at that last part, or maybe both. I walked over to my soon to be daughter and lifted her off the chair she was standing on to do the dishes, or her rendition of it anyway.

I held her close and kissed her forehead. "I would love to be your dad." She wrapped her little arms around my neck and crept that much deeper into my heart. I ignored the other half of her statement and pretended like that shit wasn't fucking with my head. How the fuck does a sweet little four year old know what mean is? I'll break his fucking neck.

Maybe I was blowing things out of proportion. Maybe he just talked loud and yelled a lot. Most kids see that as being mean right. It doesn't necessarily have to be the other thing. I still couldn't wait to get her alone to grill her ass though, and she better not bullshit me either.

I got my chance when the kids went to get ready for the park. "What the fuck did that asshole do to those kids?" She got jumpy real quick. "Nothing, he just never really had anytime for them that's all." She wouldn't look at me and the damn kids were already coming back down the hallway.

"We're not done with this." I now understood how mom used to go from batshit crazy to smiling neighbor in seconds. We both changed our facial expressions as soon as the kids came into the room. I made a big production of getting them to the car and loading the mutt into his seat in the back with the window down. I'm not sure who made the most racket, him or them.

STARTING OVER

They tired my ass out while that one sat on a bench reading a magazine. The fuck, navy training ain't got shit on these kids let loose in the park with that damn dog. I think I'm going to be one of those nervous dads. The type who panics if he loses sight of his kid for more than five seconds. Each time they ran after the dog I was hot on their tails. Lotta fucked up people in the world and I'm not legitimately cleared to off a motherfucker on domestic soil.

By the time it was almost time for her to go to work I was ready for a damn nap. The three musketeers fell asleep in the truck. Somehow the mutt ended up between the two of them on my damn seat. He knows better. Oh, what the hell they were too cute. The dog's head was in Tiana's lap and Dylan had an arm over his rump. I see a bond formed in doggie hell. I always knew my mutt was only just waiting for the right kids to come along and release the terror in him. I'ma have to build them some kinda playhouse in the back before they fuck up my shit.

***
JULIE
***

I'm too happy. I kept telling myself that while I drove into work with him behind me in his truck. My hands gripped the wheel as I fought the nerves in my tummy. It's not normal to be afraid of happiness, but I've learned over time that for each day of happy I get five of not so much. Fingers crossed that this time will be different.

He'd told the kids that we were getting married but had yet to discuss it with me. That was the reason for my angst. I don't think he'd lie to them about a thing like that, but if true, it was not what I'd expected the outcome of this little reunion to be. Would I give my eyeteeth to marry him? You betcha; but is it what's best for me, and my kids?

They loved him, that was obvious and he certainly seemed to have a fondness for them, but was it enough? I couldn't put them or myself through the hell of their dad again, and I'm not a hundred percent sure that Kevin can ever get past the fact that they're not his. I remember very well his words to me about owing him two kids. Did that mean he resented my kids?

2 | STARTING OVER

But how can he when he treats them so well. I smiled when I remembered Tiana's announcement once we got back from the park and he'd helped me clean her up before putting her down for her nap. She'd opened her tired little eyes, as he was about to lay her head on the pillow, her arms wrapped around his neck. "I'm gonna call you daddy." She fell asleep right after her little announcement, but it was his reaction that brought tears to my eyes now.

He'd looked shocked at first, then he'd blushed, then he'd ran his hand over her hair and leaned down to kiss her cheek. I'd slipped out of the room silently even though I wished I'd caught the moment on camera.

He didn't say anything when he came out of her room, just mumbled something about work to do in his office and disappeared. Now we were headed for the restaurant. I'd finally called Sandy and told her where I was. Of course she had a million questions but I told her I'd tell her all some other time. This conversation was going to need a couple bottles of wine at least.

She seemed to accept that and was just happy that I was with her brother. I don't know why I'd been so worried about it, she acted almost as if she'd known or seen it coming. He opened my car door once I parked in the lot closest to the door where he'd directed me. "From now on this is your spot." It said reserved and was the closest to the door.

I didn't question just followed him. Sandy swooped in as soon as we cleared the door. "Geez it took you long enough to get here." She dragged me away from her brother who just waved me off when I looked back at him. "Come I have a lot to show you and Mr. Impatient seems to think it can all be done in a day."

"What're you talking about? I thought I was through training?"
"Not for this you haven't."
"I still don't know what you're talking about."
She dragged me into an office. 'Ta da. Your new office." I stood in the doorway speechless. "What's going on?" She grinned and dragged me into the room and over to the desk.

"Didn't he tell you? Well, big brother calls up and says to me, 'I need a position for Julia at the restaurant. I says, 'she already has one, waitress. He says, 'that's dead find her something else in back of the house.' Well we already have a day manager, a night manager a general manager and an owner and I knew he wasn't talking about a cook. So I told him so and he says, 'well she'll be me when I'm not there.' And I said, 'the owner?' and he says 'yes' and hangs up the phone. And that's how I knew there was something going on for sure-sure before you called."

I'd followed every word she said but it wasn't registering. "I still don't…" I was starting to get a headache.

"Come I'll show you." She booted up the computer and opened files and excel spreadsheets and my hands started to tingle. Kevin was putting me in charge of his restaurant. I looked up at her to ask if this was a joke, but she was serious as a judge.

'These are all the finances for the restaurant. Order sheets, suppliers, this list here keeps track of what comes in and when we're low or need to order more of something. You'll meet with the head chef at least twice a week to discuss whatever it is they discuss. Oh and Tuesdays and Thursdays are our big delivery days, but one of the managers and the general manager, me, usually handle that. You just have to walk around and flick your whip to keep us all in shape."

There was no anger in her voice but I still felt uneasy about taking a position that would practically make me her boss. "I don't know about this Sandy. Shouldn't you be getting this job? How about we switch?"

"Are you crazy? First of all, I'm just the sister you're the woman he's in lurve with. Secondly you couldn't pay me to do this shit too much work. I signed on to help the bastard get the business up and running and three years later my ass is still here. I have enough to do thank you. Have fun and I'll see you at break time. I hear the boss coming."

She left and left me sitting there wondering if I'd really woken up this morning or if this was all part of an extended dream. "You all settled in, she showed you what you needed?" That voice, that look, that body. All real. "Yes she did but are you sure you wanna do this?" He walked over and caged me in with his hands on either side of the chair.

"Yes. Now I have to be somewhere for a few hours I'll be back." He kissed me one quick peck on the lips and left. I felt the smile begin deep in my heart and spread across my face, still I was too nervous to hope.

I got lost in what I was doing, happy to be able to put my knowledge to good use. Not that there was anything against waitressing but this was more my speed. In the background behind the scenes.

My chirping phone brought my head up and I fished around in my bag for it without looking. I had a fleeting thought that it might be one of my parents who I hadn't spoken to since they refused to let me and my kids come stay with them. As far as they were concerned my place was with my abusive husband and the divorce was all my fault.

"Hello."

"I want to see my kids."

"When?"

"Now, today."

"I'm at work…"

"I don't care where you are I want to see them NOW." Has he been drinking this early in the evening? I got that queasy feeling in my gut and that tinny taste of fear sprung in my mouth.

I took a few deep breaths and reminded myself that I was no longer attached to this asshole; except for the kids we shared that is. "Where are you?" Maybe I can buy some time and work it out to see him another day.

"I'm in your little bullshit town, at your parents as a matter of fact." The bottom fell out. That was right around the corner from where the kids were. I was never so scared in my life. Did he know?

"Fine, I'll meet you at the little diner in Copley Square." It was almost time for my break anyway. He agreed and I grabbed my bag and headed out the door. I passed Sandy in the hall coming to get me. "Hey what's your hurry?"

STARTING OVER

"I can't stop now I gotta go. I'll be back before my break is over." I hope. I wasn't planning on sticking around my ex for too long. I peeled out of the parking lot and headed for the diner. I knew it wouldn't last; gets me every time.

Chapter 20
JULIE
***

I pulled into the diner and parked having second and third thoughts about going in. I saw that his luxury car was already there and shored up my courage to get out and face him. It would be the first time since I snuck out of the house months ago, the day after I'd filed the divorce papers. It felt like a million years ago now since I'd made that decision.

I stepped out into the afternoon sun and pushed my purse strap higher on my shoulder. Inside I found him at a booth in the far back and made my way over there. "What are you doing at my parents' house?" I didn't even want to sit across from him.

Seeing him now after the last few days with Kevin I wondered what the hell I'd done to myself. I couldn't regret my kids, but I sure as hell bemoaned the fact that he was their dad. Kevin had shown them more love in the last couple days than he had their whole lives, which was pretty pathetic.

"Since when do you question what I do?" In the past those words would've sent fear racing through me because I knew what was coming next. Now I fought back the fear and stared him in the eye.

"Since we're no longer married and you never visited them even when we were." I finally sat on the edge of the seat farthest away from him. "About that... I think that was a mistake. There isn't going to be any divorce."

"Sorry but it's already final."

"Yes but we can remedy that. We wouldn't need a big wedding this time, just a trip to the courthouse."

"I'm not marrying you. Now what is it that you really want? You never had any interest in the kids before."

"I want my family back. Do you know how stupid you made me look, sneaking off in the night like that? People are talking."

"Did you forget that I have information that could put you away for a long time?"

"You'd never use it, it would destroy the children's lives and you'd never do anything to hurt them." Was that a sneer on his face? What an ass.

"Actually I think having you around them would do that. If you want to see the kids I'll make sure they're ready tomorrow." He wasn't too pleased and I could see him thinking really hard about what to say next. Obviously he thought he still had the power to cower me, and that his threat would've brought me to heel. And it might've had it not been for Kevin.

Thinking of him brought a smile to my face, which fell right off when I saw Ty walk in. He did a double take when he saw us, gave Robert the stink eye and walked over to our table even though I prayed hard that he wouldn't.

"Hey Julie, the boss know you're here?" He lifted his brow at me and I cleared my throat and rushed to make introductions before he said too much. "Tyson this is my ex-husband Robert." He didn't offer his hand just sized him up like he was taking notes.

"Uh-huh, enjoy your lunch." He started to turn away when Robert reached over and grabbed my hand. "Who the fuck is that guy?" I tugged my hand away and begged Ty with my eyes not to say or do anything when he turned back and looked at Robert like he was going to strangle him. I was afraid I knew who he was calling when he put his phone to his ear as he walked away.

"I'll call you tomorrow with a time to see the kids." I jumped up from the table before he could waylay me and wasn't at all surprised when Ty followed me out the door to my car, without a word.

I was more nervous returning to the restaurant that I had been going to meet Robert. The way Kevin talks it didn't take a rocket scientist to figure out how he felt about my ex and any relationship we might still have.

My phone rang again and I read the readout this time. My heart jumped when I saw that it was him. "Go home, I'll meet you there." He hung up and I made a U-turn and headed back to his place. Oh man he sounded pissed.

The kids were already in bed and Tracy was in the den watching a movie. "Oh you're early did something happen?" She must've seen the look on my face. I shook my head.
"No, everything's fine."
"Oh cause mom called earlier asking if you were her, she thought something had happened to one of the kids."
"Oh no, I just had an errand to run."

We both heard her uncle pulling up and she started gathering her things to leave. They met at the door and said goodnight but he only had eyes for me. I had the sudden urge to run and as soon as Tracy was gone I took off. He came after me, running. Oh shit.

I made it to the bedroom but the pocket doors were too wide for me to slam them shut before he got there. He pushed them open and I stepped back and into the room. When he turned and closed them I knew I was in trouble.

STARTING OVER

I kept backing up and he pointed a finger at me. "Stop fucking moving." I needed to pee. Why the hell do I always need to pee when I'm nervous? And why wasn't I even a little bit scared? Well that's not technically true. My heart was beating the hell out of my chest, but I didn't have that sickening fear I always got with Robert.

He didn't say anything for the longest time, just stood there watching me like he was getting ready to pounce.

***

KEVIN

***

I needed to calm the fuck down. There were kids in the house and I didn't want any part of this touching them, but she'd scared the fuck outta me. When Ty called me I'd been on my way back from meeting someone who knew a whole lot more about her ex than I'd learned thus far. What I got from that meet was that the asshole was a bully.

Bullies are weak fucks who lash out to hide the fact that they're fuckwits, very fucking dangerous. "Where were you?" I stalked her across the room until she cornered herself against the wall. "I had to meet Robert." Her eyes grew big as saucers when with my hand wrapped around her throat I pushed her back against the wall.

"What the fuck did I say?" I saw the fear in her eyes but bypassed that shit. This was about her safety, and right now I was her biggest danger. "When I tell you to do something do you think I'm talking just to hear my fucking voice? Do you need a fucking dictionary?" She shook her head and tried to pull my hand away.

"Take your fucking hands down. You're lucky you're not getting worse." She dropped her hands and tried holding my gaze. "Now let's do this again. Did I or did I not say that you weren't to meet him without my approval?" Her nose flared and I looked down at where she was biting the hell outta her lip. My dick got hard. Not the fucking time.

STARTING OVER

Then I noticed her nipples were hard and almost got diverted. "Are you fucking wet?" Her face went up in flames and she dropped her eyes. I shoved my hand down the front of her panties. Her horny ass was wet as fuck and her clit already swollen. I tugged on her panties until they tore from around her hips and fell between her feet. She lifted her hands to stop me, or some shit.

"Hands against the fucking wall behind you." She dropped her hands beside her and flattened them against the wall. Her pussy breathed on my fingers as I fucked her with them, and teased her fat clit with my thumb. I couldn't resist leaning over and taking that sexy ass mouth under mine. I pulled back as soon as she got interested.

"Now tell me again, what the fuck were you doing meeting him?"
"He wanted to talk about the kids." She was starting to get huffy. I could see her straining to hold back.
"That fucker own a phone?"
"Yes."

"Did he give a fuck about the kids when he lived with them?" I gave her a don't you fucking lie to me look.

"No." She looked away from me as if ashamed of her answer.

"Then what the fuck? You wanted to see him? Is that it? You missed being smacked around? Should I pop you upside your fucking head?" I was fishing here, I still didn't have any proof and the meet earlier hadn't even touched on that. Still I couldn't shake the feeling.

"No, Kevin...." She was shaking so hard now her knees almost gave out.

"Then what the fuck were you doing alone in a room with him?" I pulled my fingers out of her just as her body tensed to cum. I don't care which end of the monetary spectrum she comes from, you deny a woman an orgasm and she's gonna lose her fucking mind.

I'm guessing that's what the fuck was wrong with this one because of the shit that came out of her mouth next. I moved back away from her and that glazed look in her eyes went from lust to pissed the fuck off in seconds. "He's their father what do you want me to do? He has a right to see them if he wants."

STARTING OVER

I didn't answer her and I guess that infuriated that female gene that lives inside all women that makes them batshit crazy.
"And besides it's none of your business. I'm just a casual fuck remember?"
"Watch your fucking mouth."
"Fuck you."

Okay see now, I was already planning to beat her ass after that first asshole statement, but this shit just added a whole lot more pain for her ass. I grabbed the back of her head as she went to flounce past me and pulled her back. "Wrong fucking move."

Her eyes widened at my tone and I saw the fear beat like a drum in the pulse in her throat. "Oh you scared now? You should be. I'm gonna beat your ass red and put you outta my bed for being stupid. First I'm gonna fuck you because you were just in his space and that shit don't sit right with me. Then I'm gonna beat your ass red."

I took her down where she stood and mounted her, driving into her hard from behind. "Kevin, ouch."

"Shut your fucking mouth." She bit her lip and kept her complaints behind her teeth. "You're already in enough shit as it is."

She put her all into it then, pushing her ass back into me and taking my cock deep. Probably thinks that shit will make me go easier on her ass. Not a fucking chance.

"You gonna do that shit again?" I slammed into her until my balls swung against her clit. She shook her head and I stopped moving. "I want the words, so next time you do this shit I'd know you were deliberately disobeying a direct order." She stopped and fought to catch her breath.

"I won't but..."

"No fucking buts. No means no." What the fuck? Did she not hear me tell her kids that I was going to marry her ass? Did she think she was going to be my woman, living in my house, sleeping in my bed, and keeping some kind of relationship with this fuck? Not gonna fucking happen.

"I'll deal with him from now on. Understood?"

"Yes, please." She moved her ass and tried sucking my dick deeper into her snatch. She had no idea that I wasn't planning to let her cum. I slid back inside her going nice and slow while teasing her clit between the fingers of one hand while squeezing one of her tits with the other.

She clenched around my cock and my cock started to spit. I pulled out and jerked my jizz off on her back and ass before getting to my feet. "Get up." She had tears in her eyes. I have a feeling that in the future that would be all it would take for me to go easy and maybe cuddle her ass a little bit, but not today.

I sat on the side of the bed and pulled her down across my knees.

"Kevin, you can't be serious." She tried covering her ass to block me and got cum all over her hands. "Move them. The sooner you do that shit the sooner this will be over." I'd never spanked a woman before for any reason other than pleasure, never gave enough of a fuck to want to correct one. Begin as you mean to continue.

One fat tear rolled off her cheek and I pretended not to see that shit. I didn't plan on any long drawn out shit, she knew what she did wrong, now her ass would remind her for the next few hours at least. I gave her five hard whacks on her ass in rapid succession, then held my hands over the redness to keep the heat in.

She was outright bawling now but I suspected it was more from injured pride than any real pain. "There won't be a next time. You can go sleep in one of the guestrooms upstairs." She picked up her clothes off the floor and sulked her ass out the door without a backward look.

Now I'm pissed the fuck off with a hard dick. Spanking her ass made me hard as fuck but for her punishment to work I couldn't let her cum which meant I had to go without because as primed as she is if my dick gets anywhere near her she'd go off like a bottle rocket. Fuck!

I hit the shower and cooled down before jumping into bed. The shit felt empty without her like she'd been sleeping next to me for years instead of just a few nights. Turn it off Kevin. She deserved that shit. So why do I feel like a monster? Because she's got your bitch made ass bent. Shut the fuck up. On that note…

242 STARTING OVER

Sleep evaded my ass but I was too stubborn to go after her. I watched the damn clock trying to talk myself into going to get her and drag her back to bed. Was three o'clock in the morning long enough for her punishment? No. Damn.

Chapter 21
JULIE
***

I can't believe he spanked me. I thought the pain was bad while he was administering his punishment but hours later it was still stinging like hell. But that wasn't the worst of it. I'm so horny I could rub myself against the closest thing to a dick. And since when do you think like that? Since Kevin Hunt turned me into a wanton hussy.

I was tempted to go beg his forgiveness if only so he'd put out the fire between my thighs. Under my sexual frustration was the underlying memory of how hot he was in his anger. Have mercy! I had to squeeze my legs together to ease the ache. Just when I need him to take me with all that fire and manly dominance, he banishes me from his bed. He'd shown his hand though. I knew he was just as turned on as I was after his little demonstration.

The thought made me smile in the dark. Good, I hope his balls hurt. Why did I feel so safe and protected after getting my ass heated up? Maybe I have a problem after all. Whatever, I never wanted to jump Robert's stupid ass after one of his rages, but if Kevin doesn't scratch my itch come morning I just might tackle him to the floor and take what I need. I went to sleep on that thought with a smile on my face. My ass still hurt though, damn.

I woke in the morning with a dull ache between my thighs and a smile on my face, before reality came crashing back down on my head. I glared at the wall as I considered the best way to handle the situation. I could go with anger and feminine umbrage that he'd dared to spank me like a child. Okay maybe not exactly…oh never mind I have sex on the brain.

So I could go with that, or I could try something new, something daring. Something fun for once in my life. I hopped off the bed with a new pep in my step and a smug grin on my face. I brushed my teeth in the upstairs bathroom before heading downstairs.

My inner shy girl cautioned me that it was a mistake but I told that bitch to shut the hell up. I'm gonna get me some dick. Oh goodness, what the hell have I become? It's all his fault; he'd done this to me.

I heard the shower going when I walked into the master suite. He didn't forbid me from coming back here and besides I liked the tub in the master suite better than the one upstairs. I walked into the bathroom and saw him through the steamed up glass of the shower stall. He had his head under the shower, which gave me the chance to sneak past and head for the huge sunken spa tub that could hold six people.

I turned on the water while keeping an eye on the goings on in the shower. I had both taps at full blast and dropped my clothes, standing naked as I looked through the different oils and bath products he had in store. Nothing there screamed female which meant he wasn't in the habit of having women stay over. I hope.

I saw the shower door start to open and chose that moment to lean over as I tested the water. I heard his harsh intake of air and the door slammed shut. I didn't even blink though I wanted so badly to turn around. I made a big show of adding the oil I'd chosen, sniffing the lip of the bottle and sighing at the pleasant scent. My ass, I couldn't tell you what the hell I was smelling.

I tipped the bottle to pour and felt his arms come around me from behind. "I don't think you want to take a bath in my aftershave lotion." There was laughter in his voice and I wanted to die. I squinted at the bottle like I needed glasses but he already knew I didn't wear any so that was kind of a lost cause.

He reached over to the shelf with one hand while keeping the other around me. He brought back a bottle and released me long enough to open it before passing it beneath my nose. This time I read the label to make sure he wasn't trying to trick me. "You like this one?"

Dammit, I'm supposed to be the one seducing him. His dick was poking me in the ass and my itchy snatch was already on the prowl. I squeaked out a 'yes' and he poured the oil in the hot water. He lifted me into the tub before climbing in behind me. His hands covered my breasts and he nibbled on my ear.

I wanted to say 'hey, you've already tuned me up from the night before just bend me over the rim of this tub and pound it to me. I just groaned and leaned my head to the side to give him better access. One of his hands moved down between my thighs beneath the water and found my clit.

I tried opening my legs wider but his had them caged in. I pushed back into his cock that was climbing up my back, his balls teasing my butt crack. I started sneaking up sneakily, rubbing my ass on his cock as I did. His chuckle told me he knew exactly what I was doing but I didn't care. "Behave yourself. I'll give you what you want when I'm good and ready." I'll be dead by then damn.

I reached a hand back to his nape and held him close that way since it was the only part of him I could reach. That finger on my clit got lower until he was teasingly easing it into me just where I needed it. I couldn't help moving, pushing my heat into his hand, moving against his hot cock. "If you don't do something soon I'm gonna die right here in this tub."

"Are you telling me what to do with my pussy again?" He pulled my head back and drove his tongue into my mouth before I could answer. That kiss sent my temperature up a couple notches and I sucked on his tongue so hard I thought I'd hurt him when he groaned long and hard.

He rolled my nipple between his fingers and slid the other hand back down between my thighs to finger me. "Please Kevin. I need to cum." I said the words into his mouth and my heart jumped when he lifted me enough to sit me on his cock. Air left my lungs when he filled me. I had to grab the rim of the tub as he surged into me.

I bit my lip to keep myself from begging him to go faster. I know the diabolical fiend was doing it on purpose. Then I remembered, I had some power here too. I squeezed his cock with my inner walls and reached down to grab his balls. "Oh fuck!" That's right buddy two can play this game.

I fondled his balls and moved up and down on his cock, clenching and releasing until just the head was in me before sliding back down again. Now he was the one waiting with baited breath to see what I would do next. There wasn't much I could do in this position, but I worked with what I had.

I rubbed my clit and let my fingers touch the base of his cock as it stuck out of me, then on to his balls again. "Are you teasing your clit?" He looked over my shoulder at what my hand was doing and as embarrassed as I was at having him see me do that, I didn't stop.

"Yes!" For some reason that made him grab my hips and pull me down harder on his cock. Water splashed over the side wetting the floor making a mess, but I didn't care. I felt the build up and he knocked against something inside me that made my mouth drool; didn't care about that either. I just wanted that amazing feeling only he could give me.

He sped up his thrusts his tight grip on my hips getting tighter and I screamed his name as something sweet and hot rolled through my tummy down to my girly bits. My legs went numb and I thrashed around on his cock as I came harder than I ever had before. I thought for sure I was dead. He was still slamming up into me when I came back to my senses and I felt it building again. This time we came together. His growl set me off again and I was a happy girl.

***

KEVIN

***

What the fuck is she trying to do to me? At first I thought that little show in the bathroom was innocent. She wasn't the seductress type and I figured she didn't know that I was going to come out of the shower and see her fine ass bent over with just a hint of pussy showing through her thighs. Then she picked up my lotion and I got suspicious.

Now, after the fact, after I'd off loaded in her and got her off a few times, we were in the bedroom getting dressed. The kids weren't up as yet and I was giving serious thought to taking her down again when I noticed the way she moved. Her movements were slow and deliberate. How the fuck long does it take to get your leg through the leg of your panties? And who the fuck does all that wiggling and bending to do that shit.

STARTING OVER

"Hmmm, I don't think I need a bra with this top." My ass! I swallowed the pool of saliva and eyed her suspiciously. "If you plan on leaving this house you do." I didn't even see the damn top at this point. "You think so?" She turned to show me. The shit wasn't exactly see-through, but there was something about the way it was made that played peekaboo with her cleavage while her nipples tried to bust through the material covering them. Where the fuck did she get that? Very un-Julia-like.

I turned away to get dressed myself and she plopped her ass down on the bed in my view and started creaming her legs. What a production. It was all designed to make my ass crazy. It was then I caught on to what she was up to. She was paying me back for last night. I would've laughed at her efforts if the shit wasn't working.

"Come here." She flew off the bed and headed for the door.
"The kids will be up soon I gotta get breakfast ready." I heard the laughter that she was trying very hard to hide in her voice and made a grab for her.

She shrieked with laughter until I backed her against the wall, reached under her skirt and tore her panties down, released my cock, and slammed into her. I wrapped my hand around her throat to hold her in place and pounded the fuck outta her sweet cunt. I bit her lip while trying to keep her wild cries from escaping and she creamed all over my cock. Seems she likes a bit of rough play.

Her greedy pussy was on fire and I could've stayed in her all day but this was a quickie before the kids woke up so I had to get my shit together. I didn't need any special tricks to trip my trigger just one look down at her amazing face and the lust in her eyes was enough. "Cum for me baby, I'm close."

I teased her clit because women need a little more than a rutting male to get them off and she squeezed down on my cock and dragged me over the rainbow with her. "Fuck that was good." I slipped out of her and fixed myself letting her skirt drop back in place but I wasn't ready to let her go.

STARTING OVER

That hand was still around her neck and I was taking little nibbles out of her lips while pressing my cock into her middle. "You like being choked don't you bad girl?" I started to turn her to face the wall when the door behind me opened. Before I could say anything a warm little missile flew into my back. The toy fell to the floor. What the fuck.

"Don't hit my mom." I dropped my hands and stepped back as the kid flew into the room. There was fury and fear on his little face and it twisted my guts and left a bad taste in my mouth. "I wasn't going to hurt her little man." He bravely stood between us, his little body shaking as tears rolled down his face. I looked down at the toy plane he'd thrown at me to protect his mom before pulling him into my arms to offer comfort.

"It's okay buddy, we're okay."
"If you hit her we'll have to leave just like last time." What the fuck? He'd whispered the words for my ears only. I wasn't sure whose heart was racing faster at this point, his or mine.

"What do you mean?" Julie moved to take him out of my arms but I waylaid her. "We're not done here." I gave her a look that said stay put and turned back to Dylan. "What do you mean like last time?"

"When daddy hit mommy she made us leave, that's why we're here. I don't want to leave again, I like it here now." It was only because of him, his presence that I didn't fly off the handle. I turned a burning stare on her as she wrung her hands together. Not taking my eyes off her, I addressed my next statement to him.

"You're not going anywhere and no one's ever gonna hit your mom again I promise." When he wrapped his little arms around my neck and held on, it no longer mattered that he belonged to someone else. He was mine.

I took the time needed to calm his fears and tell him how proud I was of him for protecting his mom. Once his tears stopped and he was calm again I kissed his head. He's seen me do that same thing to his sister but I'd never done it to him because you know, boys. But I thought the situation called for it. I put him back on his feet and sent him after his sister.

"Go see if Tiana's awake and mom and I'll come and get breakfast ready. We've got a full day ahead of us."

"Okay…" He cut off whatever it is he was going to say and left the room. I counted to five before turning back to her. I didn't know what to do with this. When I thought it was a possibility I was pissed, but the reality was worst.

I pulled her into my arms and hugged her hard like that shit was going to change the shit that had already passed.

She held onto me and cried and I let her cry it out while I wondered if the asshole was still in these parts. There was no question I'm going after his ass and it didn't matter to me one fuck that she had been his wife. All that shit I'd been thinking and feeling since finding out the asshole she'd jumped out of my bed to marry had fucked her over died a quick death.

I covered the back of her head with my hand and pressed her closer with the other all the while asking myself what kind of spineless asshole it took to hit something that small. I wanted to knock the fuck outta something and my rage was rising by the second. I had to talk myself down. I was in a house full of children and my woman, so not the place for me to lose my shit. I wanted to hear the story but the kids were waiting. But before the day was over I'll know it all and then I'd go plant my foot in his ass.

Chapter 22
JULIE
***

I didn't know how much I needed that. I cried all over his shirt until it was soaked through and he just stood there crooning to me softly as he rubbed his hand soothingly up and down my back. I'd never really cried over my life. No one had ever looked like they wanted to kill Robert for hitting me, not even my dad. That it was Kevin doing it only made me cry harder.

We still hadn't talked about the past, but it was never more on my mind than now in the face of my complete failure. What was he thinking? He seemed to be reading my mind because he chose that moment to push my head back from his chest and dry my tears while giving me a stern look.

"Why didn't you call me?" He gritted out the words between clenched teeth. The question stumped me.

"What?" I wiped the back of my hand under my nose.

"When that fucker started hitting you, why didn't you call me for help?" How would he react if I admitted the thought never crossed my mind? "I didn't know that I could." He studied me for the longest time before dropping his hands that had been holding my hips loosely.

"We'll talk later, the kids are hungry." I rushed into the bathroom to clean my face up before following him into the kitchen. He was being so sweet, even holding my hand as we headed there. The kids were out on the deck with the dog and when they heard us coming stopped with guilty looks.

I was learning not to tense up at these situations, knowing that they wouldn't be yelled at simply for being kids, so I kept going to the kitchen while Kevin went to join the melee. The sound of my babies laughing, the dog going nuts and Kevin's soft baritone cleared the rest of the sadness from my heart as I mixed eggs in a bowl for omelets and set the bacon on the breakfast grill.

"Daddy, daddy look what I can do." I held my breath at Tiana's words and wiped my hands ready to go out there and protect her when he hurt her feelings by telling her not to call him that. "What princess, show me." I dropped down in the nearest chair in a daze.

By the time they came in breakfast was ready with the last batch of toast now popping out of the toaster. I sniffled and his eyes flew to me but I shook my head and indicated the kids, but gave him a smile to let him know they were happy tears. He gave me a weird look but said no more as he hustled the kids into the little half bath off the kitchen to wash up.

As usual the table was noisy with the kids vying for his attention and I had to tell them a thousand times not to talk with food in their mouths. Dylan was speaking so fast to outdo his sister he almost choked on a piece of toast. Tiana wanted her 'daddy' to cut her eggs for her; my services were no longer needed. It was almost like I wasn't even there.

I worried about the novelty wearing off and my tummy cramped. I looked over at him while he was paying rapt attention to something my daughter was saying to him. Tiana does this thing where she'd grab your face if she thinks you're not giving her your full attention and she did that now; with her greasy hands. It must be love because he didn't say anything to her about getting bacon grease all over his sexy face. And where did he learn to be that good with kids?

They begged for another trip to the park and he readily agreed, telling them to get their shoes on and the Frisbee to throw for the dog.
"That poor dog must rue the day these two showed up."
"He loves it, it gives him someone other than me to entertain him all day like I have nothing better to do." It must be true because as soon as he saw the Frisbee he started bounding around in circles with a happy bark.

It was getting easier to have Kevin around the kids. I thought for sure that would take some doing, but after years of hovering I was surprised to find that with him I didn't feel the need to keep an eye on them the whole time.

STARTING OVER

Just like the day before they tired themselves out and was asleep by the time we made it back to the house. We wiped them down best we could before tucking them in for a nap and he showed me in the home office how to pull up the files I needed to work on the restaurant invoices.

This was so much better than anything I'd expected. I worried how I was going to handle being away from them and not being there when they came in from school once school started back. This was the best of both worlds. I could work from home as often as I could get away with it, be here for them, and still make me own money.

That last part was very important to me. After the last ten years of someone else telling me what I could and could not buy it was going to be a joy to have my own income. Granted it probably wouldn't be much, but it would be better than what I had before.

Kevin had said he didn't want me taking Robert's money but I wasn't sure how realistic that was. I had two children to plan for, not just myself and as their dad it was Robert's responsibility to take care of their needs. Every time I think of how he tried to screw us out of what was rightfully ours, I saw red.

I earned that money for putting up with his shit and the kids deserved combat pay for the hell he put them through. I cleared my throat and looked up at him as he was busy reading some mail that was on his desk.

"About what happened this morning, what Dylan said." I risked a look at him.
"What about it?" I had his full attention now.
"I don't want you to think that they saw a lot of that. It was going on a long time, but the last time it happened, they saw and that's when I made the decision to leave."
"You think that's what I care about in this equation?"

"No, I don't know, I just don't want you thinking I'm that kind of mother." I didn't look at him, couldn't. I didn't want to see the accusation and judgment. He moved around the desk and lifted my chin. He studied my eyes for the longest time before dropping my chin and moving back around the desk.

"Why don't you tell me about this hitting stuff." The words just tumbled out. Like someone had turned the tap and rivers of water flowed. I was in tears halfway through telling him how horrible my ex had been to me, and the kids. He's the last person I would've ever imagined sharing this much of my life with, but he made it so easy. That silent stare that seemed to see into me, that said 'I'll know if you're lying so don't you fucking dare.'

He didn't say a word, just let me vent until I had it all out of my system. His mouth might not have been moving but the rage was evident in his eyes and the way he clenched his fists. "That's all of it?" When I nodded my head yes he just turned on his heel and left the room. Uh-oh, maybe I should've held some things back.

Nothing more was said and I spent the morning doing laundry and cleaning up a little. "I have a cleaning service that takes care of that. There's nothing for you to do here but take care of the kids...and me." He gave me one of those full body head to toe looks and I could almost see the smoke. Why must he be so hot? He was even better than my dreams. That only made my regret sharper.

I turned off the vacuum when he stalked towards me with intent in his eyes. My first thought was how much longer will the kids be down for their nap. He took my hand without uttering a word and led me to the bedroom and his bed. There was something different about the way he touched me. Almost like glass, like he was afraid I would break. I felt tears gathering in my eyes.

Chapter 23
KEVIN
***

I'd spent the morning after listening to her life story trying to set some things up. I wanted to hurt this guy and hurt him bad. He was already gone so I'd have to make a special trip to knock the fuck outta him and now wasn't a good time. They needed me even more than I'd first thought when I learned they were staying in that motel. And the fact that this asshole had shown up here unannounced and made demands of her told me that he had no respect whatsoever, that he thought he still had control over her life. I'm gonna have to school his ass, but there was some other shit closer to home I needed to take care of first.

I'd stayed away from her afraid that I'd hurt her with the anger that was burning through me. But seeing her looking so at home as she cleaned our house made my dick hard as a fucking steel pike and there was no denying him. He wanted to fuck. The kids would be up soon I'm sure, so I planned to do her hard and fast. But once in the room everything she'd told me came flooding back and I wanted to savor.

I wasn't ready to give her the words, wasn't ready to open myself up like that again, but I could show her with my touch. I undressed her slowly even though the clock was ticking. I was pleasantly surprised when she lifted my shirt and I raised my arms for her to pull it off over my head.

She went to work on my jeans next and I stepped out of them and my jockeys. I picked her up and kissed her as she wrapped her legs around me. I took her down to the bed and covered her body with mine. "You're so soft." I brushed a lock of fallen hair off her forehead. "And unbelievably beautiful." Her eyes were bright and full of some emotion that I couldn't quite decipher.

She took my face unsurely between her hands and brought my lips to hers. I let her take the lead for all of two seconds before her sweetness became too much and I took over. The kiss became raw and heated. Before I left her mouth with a few last nibbles of her lip and made my way down her body.

I took her breasts in my hands and squeezed gently until her nipples peeped through my fingers. "I don't pay enough attention to these I don't think. I licked first one then the other before sucking the right one into my mouth. I pressed my cock into her slit, making sure to catch her clit with the underside of my leaking cockhead.

Her pussy was already juicing as she writhed under my onslaught. She tried pulling me into her but I took my time even though I wanted inside her so bad my nuts were beginning to ache. I needed to show her, to erase the damage that had been done. She wasn't aware that I had discerned even more from our conversation than she had revealed; that I had read between the lines and knew that he had broken her down. Now it was up to me to rebuild her. She and the two kids asleep upstairs.

When her nipples became hard pebbles on my tongue I left them alone and made my way to the main course. I spread her legs open wide over my shoulders and licked the wet folds of her pussy. Her ex is an asshole. Nothing this sweet should be mistreated. How the fuck do you hold something like this in your arms and let it go?

I wasn't going to bring him here though, not even in my thoughts. I teased her clit out of hiding and slid two long fingers into her heat while tonguing her clit. "How does a pussy stay this perfect after all these years?" I may have stepped over my own invisible line in the sand with that one.

She got shy on me and tried pushing my head away. I brushed her hands aside and went back to my inspection. "Did you know you're like three different shades of pink?" Her juices overflowed into my hand and I lapped at her until there was none left. "I could eat your pussy all day, but I want to fuck you more."

She wasn't saying a word to any of this, but her eyes followed my every move. I could see the affect my words were having on her and kept it up while I climbed up her body. "Put me inside you."

I looked down as her hand moved between us and she gave my cock a few strokes before rubbing the head around her slit. When she made a pass at her hole again I pushed and slipped the head inside her tight opening. I hadn't been lying earlier. Her pussy was still as sweet as I remembered, and the memory was a lot to live up to.

"This belongs to me now. This, you the kids. After today anyone wanting to get at any of you will have to go through me." I slid deeper into her as I held her eyes. "No one will ever hurt you again, not as long as I live." I kissed the tears from her cheeks as they fell and pulled her in close, turning onto my back with my arms wrapped securely around her.

"Ride." I touched her everywhere I could reach as her body moved over mine. Soft caresses against her cheek, sweet suckling of her breasts, a tender brush of fingers up and down her tummy. And when her pussy clamped down around me like a vise, I didn't grab her ass and pound up into her the way my cock cried out for me to. But instead kept pace with her and rode the wave that washed over both of us as we came together.

When she collapsed against my chest I held her in my arms, hoping that she'd felt what I needed her to. With one final kiss to her forehead I took her from the bed and into the shower to clean her up. I even dressed her myself.

Something had changed between us, between this morning and now. Not quite sure what, it was more a feeling than anything else, but it made me feel lighter somehow. As we prepared lunch together I couldn't help but realize how different this whole thing had turned out.

After her earlier revelations I had done some serious digging. It's amazing what you can find when you start looking with different eyes. When I'd first looked into her life once learning she was coming home after getting a divorce, I'd been looking through the eyes of a spurned lover. I had my own axe to grind and quite frankly was happy as fuck that the shit had failed. Now I'm still happy, but for a different reason.

STARTING OVER

I found out some things by digging into everyone around her that I don't think even my sister knows and there's a possibility that she may not even know all of it herself. It all came about when I realized that she hadn't really known the man that had become her husband. That struck me as odd in this day and age and so I did some more searching and what I found had changed my whole perspective.

She wasn't completely off the hook, but I was feeling a whole lot more magnanimous towards her. The problem is I now have to shield and protect my little family from that shit. The best way to do that is to get my ring on her finger as soon as possible, which I plan to do soon.

The kids were starting to make noise upstairs as we were putting the finishing touches on their grilled cheese sandwiches and fruit. I looked at my watch and saw that they had been out for a little over two and a half hours. "Do they usually nap this long?"

"It depends. Today was a little hotter outside, and they ran around a lot, both of which tired them out." I'll have to remember that for future endeavors. Even the damn dog had slept away the morning. Then again his lazy ass does nothing more than sleep and chase imaginary shit in my damn yard.

Two sleepy kids came into the kitchen where they'd heard our voices still rubbing the sleep from their eyes. I noticed that Dylan was still holding his sister's hand as he led her to the table. That was a far cry from the surly kid I'd met just a few short days ago. "Hey kiddos nice nap?" They both nodded as they climbed up on their usual chairs at the table.

I tried imagining someone hurting them, especially someone who was supposed to love and protect but all that shit did was piss me off no end, so I had to put it away. It's best I focus on where we go from here. I wasn't going to try to fix his mistakes, but I was damn sure going to show them how a real man treats his woman and kids. It was scary as fuck to realize that Dylan was already mimicking some of my actions, which meant if I wanted him to grow up to be any sort of man, I'll have to be on my shit twenty-four seven.

I looked over at Julia and she looked… happier, less tense, but there was still a bit of hesitancy present. I guess that was to be expected, but I wasn't planning on letting that shit go on too long. She felt my stare and turned her head my way. I think I gave her my first genuine smile then.

Chapter 24
JULIE
***

I was telling the kids to stop playing with their food and to get a move on because it was almost time for me to be going in to work. "You're not going in today, you can work from here." He gave me a pointed look as he put a sandwich on my plate. What's with him and feeding me bread? I was only planning to have some fruit.

I looked at the bread like it was the enemy the way I'd learned to in the years I've been struggling to keep my weight down to what it was before I had the kids. That was something that had been very important to Robert, and it had become habit. I've been denying myself some of my favorite foods for years; like cheesecake.

"Are you sure?" I'm pretty sure this had something to do with what happened the night before with me going off to meet Robert, but certainly he must know I wouldn't make the same mistake twice. I preferred my ass welt free. He just nodded and dropped the subject.

STARTING OVER

He left later that afternoon and I found myself once more lounging around the pool while the kids played. I was happily surprised when Sandy showed up. It felt like ages since we'd seen each other outside of the restaurant and we hadn't really had time to talk.

"Hey you're here." She said hi to the kids and dropped down on the adjoining lounge. "Yes, my brother ordered me here. I guess he was worried about you guys being here alone, plus it's my day off anyway and I haven't got much of anything doing. The kids are all out of the house with one thing or the other and Ron is running the streets looking for some part for some manly project that goes completely over my head."

She had a bottle of wine, which she presented with aplomb making me laugh. "Hey, it's not champagne, but it's not Boone's either." That made me laugh since Boone's is what we used to drink when we first started experimenting with wine and wine coolers.

The conversation started off light but I knew there would be no better time to come clean than now. There was no question that something was going on between her brother and I, my children and I had taken up residence in his home after all, and that stunt he'd pulled with the business, was more than a dead give away.

"There's something that I never told you..." I told her the whole sordid story. The sun was about ready to go down by the time I was finished and it was time to get dinner started. She hadn't interrupted me once and when I finally did look at her face as we headed into the house behind the kids, instead of censure I saw understanding.

"And now here you are. I'm so happy for you honey. So you think big brother has an axe to grind huh."
"I guess; I mean wouldn't you?"
"But doesn't he know why you did it?" I shook my head as I pulled the chicken I had marinating from the fridge.

***
KEVIN

STARTING OVER

***

Even though I'd sent my sister to the house I still wasn't comfortable leaving them alone, so I headed back home as soon as possible. Ty had the place covered so I knew I had nothing to worry about, and the night manager was someone I trusted, well as much as I trusted anyone that wasn't part of my team.

I pulled into the garage and opened the door leading into the house. My garage is built in a way that you can't hear me coming in unless certain doors or windows are open and since it was hot as hell everything was shut up tight with the AC on full blast. So that is how I was able to walk in on their conversation without them knowing I was there.

I stopped short at Sandy's question and waited. Probably should've announced my presence but what the hell, I've learned a lot of shit at open doors before. "No, what was I going to say? Hey Kevin, I'm a complete boob who's been in love with you forever, but I have to marry this other guy because my daddy said so. But before I do, I want to give you my virginity because I never wanted to be with anyone else but you ever?"

Say what now? That was a new wrinkle. Is that what really happened or was it just something she was saying to keep my abrasive sister from lighting into her? It was obvious that she'd finally told Sandy about our night together.

"I wish you'd told him."

"What?"

"That you were in love with him, I mean, I knew. It was obvious, each time I even mentioned him you'd get all dreamy. Why do you think I was always telling you about his letters and what he was up to?"

"You knew?"

"Of course I knew, we were best friends remember? Still are." I guess the women shared some kind of girly hug then because it got quiet and then there was movement again.

"So how are things now, you two working it out?"

"Yeah, seems like. I'm not sure how to feel though. We haven't really talked about that night, not really. I used to think it didn't mean anything to him. Sometimes I'd convince myself that he never even gave it a second thought, but now I know better. My worry now, well sort of, is his relationship with the kids. Everything is new and shiny now, but what happens when the novelty wears off and he realizes that he's taken on the care of another man's kids? Will he resent them, us?"

"Are you serious? I have two stepchildren and three we share together and sometimes I forget I didn't give birth to Tracy and Nigel. If there's one thing I know about my brother it's his great capacity for love. If he didn't want your kids they wouldn't be here. You'd still be in that Motel room and he'd probably be hitting you up for sex at the restaurant. I want to thank you for sparing me that." They broke into laughter and I took that as my cue to make my presence known.

Pretending that I was just now arriving I walked into the kitchen. "What's all the laughing in here? You two got into the liquor? Where're my kids?" I didn't miss the look that passed between the two of them, or the warm flush that spread across my woman's cheeks.

"They're having some down time before dinner. You're back early." I walked over and kissed her in front of my nosy ass sister who gave me a knowing look.

"I guess this means you're kicking me out?"

"Nope, you can stay. I'll go hang with the kids until dinner's ready." I gave Julie one more kiss and kissed my sister's cheek before leaving the room. I had a lot of shit to think about after that little bombshell but first I wanted to spend some time with the kiddos.

I learned two things. One, she hadn't been using me all those years ago. And now that the truth was out there I guess I could see why she went the route she took. The truth is she could have no way of knowing that I would wake up the next morning half in love with her. And the other was that she was worried about me, and the kids. Words won't work here, so I was just going to have to show her.

That night after dinner and Sandy had left and the kids were down for the night, she was being very skittish, more like jumpy. I was about to make her tell me what the hell was bothering her when she surprised me once again. We were in the den like normal people watching some mind numbing drivel on the tube. It was the first time I hadn't jumped on her as soon as the kids were down and it was for shit.

I watched her out the corner of my eye, squirming and moving around on her chair across from me, taking peeks at me when she thought I wasn't looking. Just when I was about to tell her she better tell me what the hell was on her mind, she left her chair and walked over to me. I almost laughed when I caught on to what was going on with her.

I didn't say shit, just let her work it out on her own, almost holding my breath to see what she would do next. She climbed into my lap and put her mouth on mine. Her lips were soft and inviting. The little tease pulled back when I started to reciprocate and I pinched her ass.

She laughed and put them back again and this time ran her tongue along the seam of my lips. I opened my mouth slightly and teased the tip of her tongue with mine. She sighed into my mouth and drew my tongue into hers. I drew her in tighter with my arm around her back and deepened the kiss.

She ground her crotch down hard onto my growing dick and her body trembled slightly. I could smell her heat and feel the hard points of her nipples as they pressed into me. My hand went up under her shirt and touched her full tit wondering what the hell had set her off. There was nothing on the show that would've sparked such a reaction, so I'm guessing she just wanted her man.

"You wanna fuck baby?" She buried her face in my neck and nodded her head shyly. I was pleased as fuck that she was learning to make the first move; that she felt comfortable enough with where we are to do that. The old Julie had been shy and from what I overheard this evening had been too afraid to make a move until it was too late.

She stood as if expecting to go to the bedroom but I pulled her back down on my lap. "I'm gonna do you right here." She looked around at the wall of windows and French doors that led onto the wrap around porch. "No one can see us here babe, don't worry."

I made her strip and straddle my lap while keeping my jeans on. I removed my shirt because I like feeling her hands on me, but I wanted her to feel that little bit of vulnerability from being naked while I'm still covered.

I teased her clit with my thumb while rubbing four fingers slowly back and forth over her slit from below. She fed me one of her tits and wrapped her arms around my head when I made love to it. Her pussy was heating up and her juice coated my fingers. I pulled them away from her and licked them dry before going back for more.

She came just from that, a nice soft shiver and a moan before she revved up again. "Take him out." She dropped her hands from around my head and fought with my zipper to release by burgeoning cock. He sprung up tall and proud and looking for some pussy action. I took her ass in my hands and moved her back and forth over my cock, teasing her entrance with each slide.

"Sit on my cock and ride." I held my cock so she could lift her ass and come back down on me. I held her head with one hand and fed her my tongue while bottoming out inside her. We both held still for a second enjoying the feel of each other. When her pussy started clenching I knew she was ready to fuck so I kept that hand behind her head and used the other one to pull her on and off my cock by her ass.

She was extra saucy tonight, slamming her cunt down on my rod like he was about to become extinct. "What's gotten into you baby?" "Nothing, no, I don't know."

Chapter 25
JULIE
***

Yeah I did. He'd been so sweet all evening, with me, the kids, that somehow his masculine frame, those muscled arms that for some reason makes me hot, were extra everything tonight. The way he spoke to Tiana or touched her little head when she called him daddy, or the way he had a serious conversation with Dylan about some ballplayer that the two of them seemed googly over; males.

Or when he asked me if I had enough and tried to feed me more. I could've cried. Instead I got extra horny and just wanted to jump his bones. It was hell waiting for his sister and my friend to leave, and then bath time and the interlude before bedtime. I thought I was going to die.

Then instead of dragging me off to bed, as was his norm, he wanted to watch TV. Go figure. I was so twitchy a high wind would've made me jump out of skin. I wish I knew what that was all about; he hadn't even touched me. Well except for at the table when our hands would touch accidentally, or when we were standing together at the door saying our goodbyes to Sandy and his hand kept sliding up and down my back to my ass and staying, before doing it all over again. Yeah, I'm easy.

Now he was stuffing me so good and the way his arms felt around me, so protective, it made me feel safe and warm even while he was driving me mad with his slow powerful thrusts. This afternoon's lovemaking had been sweet and special, but I miss his overpowering dominating rip roaring sex.

I was so close, but I waned to feel his finger teasing my ass. I wanted him to bite the flesh around my nipple and leave his mark.
"Kevin."
"Yes baby." That hand he had on my hip was torture because it was holding me back from moving harder, faster. He held my head back and looked at me.

"What is it?"

"I…" I couldn't say it. My face turned red as fire and I tried to hide it in his shoulder but he wouldn't let me. "Tell me." He moved even slower now just letting me rock back and forth on his hard cock, smashing my clit into his pelvis with each forward thrust. I wanted to bite him and tell him to get on with it. I got as far as the bite when his finger touched my clit just enough to get me going.

"Ouch." I left my teeth in his chest and tried to show him what I wanted by moving my ass faster. Still I could only move around in circles because of that hand on my hip. "If you don't tell me it's not going to happen." He knew, the snake and was toying with me. Again, two can play at this game. I was enjoying this new heady approach to sex. Only with him could I feel this free to let go. I could cry for all the wasted time.

"I want you to fuck me." I made myself hold his eyes as I said the words even though I felt like I was gonna throw up. His nostrils flared and he got up and turned, bracing my back against the edge of the soft leather chair.

He grabbed both my hips and pounded into me as I held onto the chair arms for support before he sent me sliding. "Is this what you wanted?"

"Yes-yes-yes-yes-yes..." His hips were like a piston, moving in and out of me so fast it was hard to catch up. I didn't care, I could feel that tidal wave forming in me again and I wanted it, wanted that sweet release that only this man could give me.

"I'm going to cum I'm going to cum, I'm going to cum..." I have no idea why I was repeating everything. I came so hard my scream choked off in the middle and my mouth hung open as my eyes widened and the mother of all orgasms ripped through me.

He never stopped moving and the feeling rebuilt almost as soon as it was over.

"Cum on my cock again; that's it. You ready to get fucked?" Oh shit, what was that just now? If he did anymore I won't make it. He pulled out and put me on my hands and knees. He positioned me how he wanted, with a hand in my back bending me forward, his hands on my hips spreading my ass as he opened my legs wider.

He drove that fat log in me and went deep with one stroke and my girly bits got to gushing and squishing and the slight pain in my tummy where his cock was battering away at my insides was all worth it because nothing had ever felt so good.

"Oh yeah, you're in the right position for a breeding." And with those climax-inducing words, he proceeded to give me what I'd asked for. I don't think I stopped cumming once he started pounding into me from behind. My poor arms almost gave out but my knees were holding up just fine.

He had them off the floor as he held me up by my hips and plowed into me so good I was crying and drooling while my girly bits wept.
"Breed me Kevin." Oh shit.
"Hold on." My knees went back to the floor, one hand went around the back of my neck and the other gripped my hip and he slammed, bam-bam-bam...
"OH-oh-oh-oh....

I think he moved something in there and reorganized my reproductive organs but that was okay. He was as deep in me as he'd ever been and it was magic. There was pain and pleasure and love and lust and every sexual emotion beating a path through my blood. And when he slammed into me one last time as I was building to orgasm, pulled my head back roughly and shoved his tongue down my throat, I was in heaven.

No one had ever loved me that hard or that thoroughly before. I'd never felt so completely taken over, mastered, owned, and I loved it. He didn't end the kiss once we both came down and when it got too uncomfortable to hold my neck arched back like that, he pulled out and lifted me in his arms and headed for the bed.

He laid me down gently and slid his still semi hard cock back into my depths before continuing our kiss. I felt him growing inside me as our lips tangled and was surprised that I wanted more. I could feel my body heating up again and that sweet tingle started in the pit of my gut and exploded deep in my core where his cockhead was tapping away at my cervix door.

STARTING OVER

He stayed inside me all night and by the time I woke up in the morning the kids were already fed and outside playing while he sat on the deck having coffee.

Chapter 26
KEVIN
***

She damn near killed me. What the fuck! I'm thinking the asshole didn't even tap into her passion not even a little bit. So although he'd stolen ten years from me, he hadn't taken what's always been mine. But I'm gonna have to put her ass on some kind of ration. If she keeps this shit up I'll be dead inside a week. I'm sure if she were telling the story it would be the horny male that was at fault for the longest sexual marathon in creation, but it won't be true.

She was hungry as fuck last night and I forgot to ask her what the hell flipped her switch. When my dick was too soft to please her, she sat on my face while sucking me off to get him going again. When her pussy hurt because her ass was being greedy and refused to stop I fucked her ass to give her pussy a break. I must've nutted six times last night, well seven, if you count the double shot I put in her ten seconds apart.

STARTING OVER

I'm hiding out with the kids as my cover just in case her horny ass is looking for more. I'd left her sprawled out on the bed hours ago, thank fuck. My dick was now coming back to normal. I almost iced him down this morning but a little bit of ointment seems to have done the trick. I heard her moving around inside before making her way out to where I sat.

I wonder which Julie I'm going to see today. Shy reserved Julie, or sexual tigress. It didn't matter; I love them both. Yeah I can admit that to myself now. Now that I knew she hadn't betrayed me. There was only one dark cloud in my atmosphere and I was going to take care of that some time today.

She came and stood next to me, filched my cup, and took a swallow. "Hey get your own caffeine thief." She laughed and walked down to where the kids were digging in the ground. Probably looking for worms for bait. I'd had to teach my daughter not to be afraid of the squirmy little buggers after her brother tried tormenting her with one. Now she's just as dirty as he is with mud over every visible surface. Their mother's gonna have a fit.

"What in the world? How did you two get like that?" Yep.
"Dad said it was okay. Didn't you dad?" I swallowed like a bitch and answered my son. "I sure did son. Your mom's a girl they don't understand these things." I got a couple dirty looks for that one. Damn they start young.
"But daddy I'm a girl I unnerstan."
"Very true princess I stand corrected. Only moms don't understand then I guess."
No one made a big deal of Dylan's capitulation and that easily I became dad and daddy.

***

JULIE

***

I badgered him into letting me go in for a few hours that evening. With my newfound freedom I found I liked to stretch my wings, well as much as he'd let me anyway. He wasn't too happy about it but once I promised not to leave the restaurant without him to go on any clandestine meetings he caved.

Ty the snitch gave me a smirk when I walked through the door. "Tattle tale." I teased as I walked by. "You bet; the boss know you're here?"
"Oh my gosh I work here." He just gave me one of those looks that older brothers reserve for little sisters and I almost squirmed even though I knew that Kevin had given me permission.

Instead of chafing at the way Kevin and now his men were acting, I felt cossetted. I had no doubt that Kevin had put Ty up to keeping an eye on me when he wasn't around so I poked my tongue out at him like a brat and walked away. "Why don't you call him? You know you want to. He actually put his phone to his ear like he'd already dialed the number. Geez.

"Yeah she's here. Giving me a lip full." I stopped when I heard that. He held the phone out to me and I just shook my head. "Hello?" I half expected him to be joking but no such luck. "Ty's on you 'til I get there, behave yourself."
"Um, okay." I passed the phone back and he closed it with a smirk. I just huffed and walked away but inside I was tickled pink.

I got some work done before going in search of Sandy for some gossip and a break. Kevin had decided to stay home with the kids until later when Tracy was going to relieve him. I didn't even bat a lash at leaving them alone; my only worry being what state the house was going to be in when I got home tonight.

Kevin is one of those dads that believe in letting kids be kids. After they'd covered themselves in mud looking for worms they'd rolled around with the dog some before sitting down by the pond to fish. My dainty little girl was right there in the middle of them keeping up with her daddy and her big brother. Of course Kevin slowed down enough to make that possible, but it was the cutest thing.

I spent more time with Sandy than I'd intended before heading back to the office, now mine and Kevin's. If I were watching a movie I would find this all preposterous. People didn't find their happily ever after in real life. And certainly not like this, so fast it'll make your head spin. But here we were.

I only got a little worried when I thought of Robert's next visit or interruption, but even that no longer had the power to scare me like it did just a few short weeks ago. Then there were my parents and that whole situation. It was only a matter of time before they knew I lived around the corner from them, or we ran into each other. Awkward!

I came around the corner and came up short when I heard his voice. It was the tone that gave me pause, he sounded pissed. Then I heard the other voice and my vision went red. I felt a rush of possessiveness so strong it almost knocked me to my knees.

"She'll never be woman enough for you. I know what you like." Said the serpent.
"Oh yeah, and what's that?" Couldn't she hear the menace in his voice?
"I remember the games we used to play…" I started to move forward but my legs seemed stuck in place.

"With you it was a game with her it's real. Get in here legs." How does he do that? Natalie stepped away from him with a venomous look thrown my way when I stepped into the room. I was spitting mad and ready to scratch her eyes out. It's obvious that she'd had her hands on him.

"Easy there tiger." He wrapped his arms around me and swung me around and away from her. I can't believe I almost hit her. "I don't think I can work here if she's here." That's about the meanest thing I've ever done in my life. I felt bad saying it, but if he wouldn't even let Robert see his kids without him there, I don't see why I should accept someone he'd slept with.

"She's gone."
"Excuse me, I have employee rights you can't just fire me because this bitch said so."
"Well baby, you're the owner what do you say to that?" I felt ten feet tall in that moment. "Sounds like grounds for termination to me. You're fired. I'll call someone to cover the rest of your shifts." I actually gave her a little finger wave and Kevin picked up the phone to call Ty.
"I need you to escort Natalie off the premises. If she damages anything call the cops."

She stomped out the door in a fury and I was glad to see the back of her. "Hey baby; what were you and my sister up to?"
"How do you know that's where I was?"
"I know everything you do." He pulled me in and kissed me on the cheek. "You ready to go?"
"I'm leaving? I just got here."

"Yeah but I don't like the atmosphere around here tonight, you're going home." I pouted but there was no waylaying him. What did he mean by that by the way? Did he expect Natalie to cause problems?

She was already gone when we got out front and from the looks of Ty there was some kind of showdown. He had a scratch down one side of his neck and a murderous look in his eyes. "What the hell happened to you?" Kevin stopped us in front of him.
"I laughed at Natalie's fired ass." He looked down at the scratch. "It was worth it." He shook his head and grinned at Kevin and I wondered what secrets the two of them were keeping.

***

KEVIN
***

Well, well, well, my little tigress has claws. It was amazing to watch her coming out of that shell and hitting her stride. Hopefully I had something to do with this new confidence she had. If last night was anything to go by she was finally coming to accept her place in my life. I hadn't officially asked her to marry me yet I was waiting to buy the ring first and then put it on her finger before dragging her before the altar. I wasn't getting down on my knees though; fuck that.

"Who the fuck is that?" There was a strange car in the driveway. The phone rang and my niece's number showed up. "What's up kid?" "Uncle Kevin you need to come. There're these two men here and they say I have to let them have the kids." I jumped out the truck and hit the ground running with her hot on my heels.

Tracy met us at the door with the phone still in her hand. The kids were huddled together on the couch looking scared as fuck and the dog was standing guard and pitching a fit. But a quick scan of the room showed that it was empty except for them. "What's going on? Julie asked at the same time I asked 'where are they?'

STARTING OVER

"They went around back when I wouldn't open the door." I pulled her into my chest but my eyes were on my kids. "Good girl. Take the kids upstairs. You go with them too baby this won't take but a minute." She looked like she was tempted to disobey me but common sense took over in the end and she followed looking back at me every step.

I kept my cool until they were out of sight and then reached in my back for my glock. I tracked them around the back of the house. I hit the outside lights and pulled the door open at the same time gun pointed.

"What the fuck, are you doing on my property?" I stepped outside and closed the door behind me. The asshole ex didn't see the gun since he was behind her dad and started to puff up his chest. "I came to get my kids…" He stared at the gun and looked at the older man and back to me.

"There's no need for all that, put that thing away." Her dad, Frank if I remember correctly was looking a little green himself. "I asked you what the fuck you were doing here. You." I pointed at the ex. "You and me, we're gonna tango but not here, not now. Not with my woman and kids around. But I know where you live. As for you, your daughter's been home more than a week, has been living here right around the corner from you for a few days and haven't even thought of calling or coming to see you. I'm thinking that means she doesn't want to."

"If that should change and she decides that she does I'll think about letting her and our kids be anywhere near you."

"Just who do you think you are? You have no rights over my daughter and grandchildren. He's their father, her husband..."

"Where were you when this asshole was beating on her? You're no dad and you're not going to be a grandfather to my kids."

"Your kids?"

"Yes mine and I'll fucking shoot anyone who says different. Julie, go inside." I'd heard her come out behind me but didn't take my eyes off these two fucks. I didn't want her anywhere around the asshole ex and the dad was a close second on that deal.

"How could you come back here and play the whore with this, this...?" I put my hand on the trigger and barely restrained myself from shooting her dad in the head because of the three kids in the house. "Julie inside, now."

She didn't even balk, just walked her ass in the house with her head held high. I know I was gonna pay for this later but whatever. It was high time someone put his overbearing ass in his place.

"You sold her ten years ago. No don't get scared she doesn't know and she never will, but if you ever in your miserable fucking life talk to my woman like that again I'll drop you. Now go the fuck home and be thankful I'm not cutting you off completely. I'd have to explain that shit to her and I won't do that to her. But just remember, I'm watching you, with her *and* my kids." The weak fuck, who likes to beat up on women hadn't said fuck one since he saw my piece pointed in his direction. Asshole is queer as a football bat.

"Go, before I change my mind." They made tracks getting the fuck outta my space and I was mad as fuck that I'd finally come face to face with the asshole ex and couldn't do shit. It was more important for me to go reassure and comfort my family.

"Fuck!" She was standing just inside the door hidden by the wall and from the look on her face I could tell that she'd heard everything.

"Come here baby." I opened my arms and she flew into them. "What did you mean when you said my dad sold me to Robert?" "We'll talk about it later baby, let's go see about the kids." Before I could turn her towards the stairs there were screeching tires out on the driveway and I thought the assholes had come back with reinforcements.

I looked at the security monitor and saw Ty, Marshall another one of my guys, and my brother in law Ron. All three men were loaded for bear. "What the fuck?" I opened the door as they came rushing in guns drawn.

"Tracy called Sandy, Sandy told Marshall and me and then called Ron, where are they?" Just then my niece came bounding down the stairs and straight into her daddy's arms. My little princess peeped out from behind her brother with her thumb in her mouth. I'd never seen her do that and can only surmise that she did it when she was afraid or nervous.

I got down low and opened my arms for her and she flew into them. "It's okay princess daddy's got you." I gave the guys a quick rundown of the situation and of course they wanted to stay, even though I told them we were fine. I was talking to air. Ron took a shaken Tracy home and Sandy was ringing my phone off the hook.

I left the guys and took Julie and the kids to the master bedroom. Dylan had been quiet this whole time and once we got there and I got them settled on the bed I directed my statement to him. "You two will sleep in here with us tonight." I know some fucked in the head shrink somewhere would say this was a bad idea, that it was setting a bad precedent or some fuck, but I didn't give a fuck what some coked up quack had to say about how the fuck I choose to raise my kids.

Dylan seemed to relax a little and I didn't miss the fact that he was holding his sister's hand. "You two were scared huh. It's okay to be scared, but you did just right. You listened to Tracy and stayed calm, I'm proud of you both." Tiana gave me a sleepy smile. Poor baby was plumb tuckered out. And Dylan lost that haunted look from his eyes.

I hugged my woman and whispered reassurances in her ear. "Baby, whatever happened ten years ago is in the past. We're here now and nothing's going to change that. Let me go tell these two that we're fine here and I'll be back."

I left her with the kids and went back out to where the boys were standing on my deck with the dog, who was on high alert. "Guys, thanks for coming but you can go now. We're good here." "No can do Cap. We're staying. Why don't you go on inside with your family. Marsh and I will take shifts." What the fuck, this isn't Mosul.

Ty was in Op mode, which means he's not going anywhere no matter what I say. Even as their leader, when it comes to my safety they'd ignore even me. That's what I get for training them too well. "Fine, I see you've already found the beer and you know where the spare rooms are." I left them and the dog and headed back inside.

She was in bed cuddling the kids who were fast asleep. There were tears in her eyes and dry tracks on her cheeks. I eased Tiana out of her arms and pulled her out of bed. I carried her to the chaise lounge in the sitting room and sat with her in my lap.

She cried silently as she clutched my shirt in her fists. "How did you find out?" I kissed her temple and squeezed her. "I ran your ex and some things didn't add up. So I went deeper. It didn't make sense to me that your dad was so dead set on you marrying this guy who you didn't even really know. I couldn't see where any of that made sense. Your dad was having some financial difficulty and his dad needed a blind for him."

"He was constantly getting into trouble and causing a scandal of one sort or another, and they figured if he settled down with a wholesome all American beauty it would give his look some polish. Your dad just happened to be friendly with his, and was in need at the time so you drew the short straw. Now I want you to take the time to get over the hurt of that, but I also want you to keep in mind, if none of this had happened, you wouldn't have those two in there. So whenever you start to feel bad about this mess, remember that. Think only of them."

"But we lost so much…"
"I know baby, but we can't get it back and there's no point in mourning the fact. We're here now older and wiser. And I love you." I felt her body jump, but carried on with what I was saying. "I couldn't love you more than I do right this minute. So ten years later or not, we've found each other again."

She didn't say anything for the longest time, just ran her hand up and down my chest and then she picked her head up and looked into my eyes. "You love me."

"Well yeah!" She grinned and gut punched me playfully before putting her head back on my shoulder. "You'll be okay princess."
"I thought Tiana was your princess."
"She is, and so is her mother and the sisters she's soon to have."
"When you say sisters, how many were you thinking?"
"Well now. I'm thinking you gave the asshole one of each so you have to give me two of each at the least."
"You do realize I'm thirty-one I'd have to have a kid a year for the next four years or I'll be having babies well into my forties."
"Well then I suggest you get on that shit right quick."

Chapter 27
JULIE
***

The man is a tyrannical menace. It's been three days since the little home invasion and I don't think the kids and I have been allowed to be on our own for one waking moment. If Kevin wasn't here, then one of his team was. If I even moved towards the door someone was there, blocking my way before I turned the knob.

Our trips to the park were more like an exercise in secret service training. At least it was good for some comic relief. Three grown men trying to keep up with my little whirlwind and playing twenty questions with her brother while trying to corral a rambunctious dog was just too much.

Today I was getting a breather. Kevin had lit out early with some obscure statement about having to go out of town for a meeting. Still I was confined to the house and his parting words, 'your ass better not step one toe out this bitch until I return' pretty much said it all.

I spent the morning keeping the kids busy. I'd had days to think of the revelations about what my dad had done in the past, and whenever I was feeling down about it I climbed into Kevin's lap and cried on his shoulder until I got it out of my system. Then he'd make love to me slowly, tenderly, until I cried tears of a different kind.

Those encounters were all well and good and certainly needed at the time, but I was beginning to miss my crazy man. Tonight the kids were going back to their beds no matter how my daughter bats her lashes at her daddy to con him into staying in ours. I knew they were over whatever trauma they'd suffered that night and were now just milking it for all it was worth. It was too cute to see them play him, and even more amazing that it were possible.

They might be suffering from the same whiplash as I, going from Robert's bullshit indifference to someone who actually cared about them and what they felt. He never once shut them down in the last few days no matter how silly the question and they were way ahead of me in fully accepting our new life.

I still had moments when I wanted to pinch myself, when I couldn't believe that this was all real. He tells me he loves me all the time now and each time it's like winning the jackpot. There are really no words to describe what it feels like to have the man you adore with all your heart say those words to you when he's buried deep inside you as he looks deeply into your eyes.

Crap; time to change my thinking here, I just slightly came on myself. I found Tyson in the kitchen making more coffee while Marshall was telling the kids a story about one of his Ops with their dad. Their eyes were big as saucers so I was sure he was laying it on thick to make Kevin look good. Not that he needed much help there.

"I'm going to sit out back and get some sun is that allowed?"
"Let me check with the boss." He had to be kidding. I rolled my eyes and left the room to the sound of his laughter.

***
KEVIN
***

I timed it well arriving at his home when I was sure he was there. She didn't know that he'd lost his job and was two steps away from being broke. He didn't even know that he was almost broke. Except for the ten dollars I'd left in his account when I used my clearance to find it where he had it stashed away in the Caymans. He'd be finding the shit out soon enough.

I'd put the money in a trust for the kids and when the time comes they'll know where it came from and can decide if they want to keep it or not. But their care was coming out of my pocket from now on.

He was in his kitchen moving shit around in the cupboards and muttering shit about a worthless bitch, who I presume is my future wife. That's grounds to put a cap in his ass right there, but I had some shit I wanted to tell this fuck before I fuck his shit up.

STARTING OVER

I waited for him to even sense my presence but he didn't have a clue. Amateur. I got so far as pulling a chair at the table and sitting down before he knew I was there. Coulda dropped this ass and buried him out back already. He almost shit a brick when he turned with coffee bag in hand and saw me sitting there watching him.

I didn't have my gun out this time. Never bring a glock to a kiddie rubble. I wasn't even dressed the part. Sweats and a hoodie and some sneaks, he didn't warrant ass-kicking gear. Pansy ass motherfucker.

"What are you doing in my kitchen?" Good for you; show some bravado that way I know I'm not about to knock the shit out of a female. Thought for sure this bitch was missing his balls, but I guess the two kids disprove that theory.

My arms were folded over my chest and I guess his eye fuck was to ensure there was no gun. "I told you we needed to talk." Fucker jumped a foot in the air when I stood, and backed away. "I don't know what she told you but it's all lies."

"Really? You never took your fists to her? You didn't terrorize two kids that were depending on you for love and security?" Is this guy on something? His eyes moved from side to side like a damn rodent. Way fucking off. "Look, I worked hard, I wasn't here enough…"

"Not interested in your lying ass history. I want something from you. It's the only thing that's going to save you from an early grave." I drew the papers from the small of my back where I'd shoved them when I left the truck.

"What's that?"

"You're going to sign these giving up all rights to my kids and then I want you the fuck gone out of their lives forever. Before you say anything, this isn't a fucking debate. Your signature or your blood; choose!"

"That's blackmail, that's, that's extortion."

"I think the word you're looking for is coercion college boy, and yes, yes it is. What you gonna do about it? I can do you one better. That shit that she threatened to take to the media, nothing stopping me from doing that shit."

STARTING OVER

The asshole swallowed hard before reaching for the papers. "You got a pen?" I gave him one and watched him sign with distaste. I'd have died before I signed away my fucking kids I don't give a fuck if you had the three hundred behind you.

I took the signed papers and read the signature to be sure he wasn't pulling a fast one. "Now that that's done." I put them away and reached for him, lifting him off the floor by his neck. "Hey I thought you said..."

"Shh, snowflake, I'm not gonna kill you. I'm gonna beat you to within an inch of your life but you'll survive. And guess what, I know where to hit so it doesn't show." I squeezed down on his jugular until his eyes damn near popped out of their sockets before slamming him into the wall.

I hit him with the Z, hitting every pressure point in his body. That way he'd think he was dying and the fear and pain will linger for a while after I'm gone. I dropped him to the floor where he was fighting to breathe and leaned over into his face. I kicked his legs apart and planted my foot on his balls. "Don't ever come back to my town. You come anywhere near my family they'll never find you." I ground my heel into his nuts until I heard the little pop and walked out the door to the sound of his high-pitched screams. Fuck yeah that was good.

Chapter 28
KEVIN
***

I was back in time to take my kids to the park. That night I convinced my two shadows that it was okay to leave their posts. I had to pull rank to get their asses out of my house. But I needed my woman tonight and these little quiet fuck sessions weren't cutting it.

I didn't tell her what I'd been up to that morning though her suspicious ass kept giving me looks. I waited until the kids were down and the house was quiet. The fucking dog who knew he wasn't allowed to sleep inside and had his own house, refused to leave so now he was standing guard upstairs with the kids. I'm a bitch in my own house now. Everybody's just running my shit.

"What is this?" She unfolded the papers I dropped on the bed next to her.

"One is the papers your…the kids…Robert the asshole signed giving up all rights to the kids." I didn't know what the fuck to call him. "The others are the adoption papers." She looked up at me like she didn't know what to say or think and then the tears started.

Dammit, there goes my pussy. Can't very well mount her like a rutting beast if she's crying and shit. I pulled her up and into my arms and let her blubber all over me. "Are you upset, happy, what? Help me out here." She nodded her head like that shit made sense.

"Which one?"
"I'm so…I'm so happy." Happy was one long drawn out word and the blubbering shit started again and I rolled my eyes like a distressed teenage girl. "You done?" She nodded against my chest as the sniffling tapered off.
I needn't have worried about the pussy because after she was through with the tears, she damn near took me down.

STARTING OVER

There's nothing like a reserved woman cutting loose. I don't know what it was. Maybe it was the knowledge that the asshole was completely out of our lives, or the fact that I wanted to adopt the kids; but something unleashed the freak in her. Lucky me.

She had me stripped with my cock in her mouth while she knelt between my legs next to the bed, and I sat with my hands grabbing fistfuls of her hair. Even her throat was in the game because she didn't gag not once while she was taking my shit down deep. "Fuck!" Her nose was buried in my groin and my cock was doing a happy dance in her neck.

When she almost sucked the skin off my rod with her greedy shit I pulled her off and threw her to her back on the bed with her legs in the air and dove headfirst into her pretty pussy. "You shaved." Her pussy was smooth and pink. I ran my hand over the soft flesh, opening and closing her slit like a fish mouth while fucking with her clit until her juices started seeping out.

I licked her cream into my mouth and went back for more. She fucked herself on my tongue and tried to scalp my ass as she pulled me into her cunt by my hair. I drank from her well until I had my fill and my cock was getting ready to launch a revolt. I kissed her inner thigh and got to my knees spreading her legs wider to take me.

I slammed into her so hard I thought I'd hurt her, but the wild movements of her hips as she came on my cock told me she was fine. I fucked her through her climax and once she came down nuzzled her lips until she opened for my tongue. When she bit my lip I knew just what she needed. I was right there with her. The last couple nights of quiet sex because we had a houseful of people had left me hungry.

"I want you from behind get on your knees for me baby." I pulled out and tapped her on the hip to get her moving. She hopped into position and I had her hair fisted and my cock balls deep before she had her hands planted in the bed. I fucked her for all the years I'd missed. All the years of mediocre when this was out there.

STARTING OVER

I put my hand on her tummy right where I was hoping my kid was already growing and drove into her over and over again. She got sneaky and screamed out 'I love you' when I was too far-gone but I heard that shit and answered. "I love you more."

When I came this time it was with something more than raw lust. All the love that had been waiting inside for her poured out of my into her as I held her close with my chest to her back and my arms wrapped tightly around her.

I spent the rest of the night doing my best to breed her if I hadn't already. That night I made a promise to her and myself that they would never know another moment's worry. Not if I could help it.

She laid on my chest and told me all that was in her heart and had been since she was a young girl, and I promised to treasure her love and never give her reason to regret it. Damn, has it really only been a little more than a week since she moved in with me? It felt like a lifetime.

Epilogue
KEVIN
***

I gotta get outta this house before I lose my mind but I'm running out of excuses. I've fixed everything that needed fixing, the nursery was done to her specifications and the fridge was full of the nasty shit she can't live without. She waddled by me in these new stretchy things that was all she lived in these days and this cute top that molds her round belly and my dick caught her scent.

I eyed her ass and cursed myself for being a sick fuck. She was ready to pop and all I could think was how fucking hot she looked in her last month of pregnancy. Fucking setup. I want her all the time, but I'm so afraid to hurt her that I dare not risk it.

Instead of my ardor cooling it only seems to get worse. She grows more beautiful everyday, which I would've never thought possible. I've seen pregnant women before and none of them ever made me lose my shit. I just get a whiff of her and I'm ready to hump her ass like a stray mutt.

She's like, a walking miracle or some shit. She's carrying my kids, taking care of our other two and still looks like she can take on the world. Then at night she rolls into bed smelling and feeling like the best of everything in my life. And I can't have her. Fuck!

She bent over to put something in the garbage and those stretchy pants pulled tight across her fine ass and I slammed down my can of pop and stormed out the door. A few hundred laps should do me good. I headed for the pool stripping my shirt off over my head as I went. I kicked off my jeans when I reached the pool and dove in.

I pushed myself until my arms started to burn. When I pulled myself up on the side she was sitting there waiting for me. She held a towel out for me but I knew that's not why she was out there. She had something on her mind.

Her tits were about to bust out her top and I put my head down and counted to five before climbing out the water. I wrapped the towel around my waist and looked everywhere but at her.

"What's up baby, the kids kicking?" She leaned back on her hands and everything was on full display. Now I was fixated on the vee between her thighs. My cock was starting to tent the towel so I sat on the chair next to hers. "Julie I'm talking to you." I've been on full alert since she started showing. I notice everything about her and am always trying to put out fires before they start.

I get the kids up in the morning for school, pick them up in the evening and I've even eased her out of working without her realizing it. She didn't sneeze without me knowing and I'm right there with the tissues.

She rubbed her tummy and smiled but there was still something in her eyes that I didn't like. I can't stand to see even a hint of sadness in her; it tears me up inside. According to Sandy, I'm suffering from my wife's pregnancy hormones. There've been a few murmurings down at the restaurant, but I mostly ignore that shit. So what if I'm not the first man to have a pregnant wife, she was my wife dammit and this shit was scaring the piss outta me.

STARTING OVER

I stay awake at night gritting my teeth and going through the route to the hospital over and over in my head. Once or twice I've made the dry run and had my boys timing that shit and giving me pointers for improvement. I now have my brother in law on speed dial because he's my go-to guy for birthing questions. He was in the room with my sister with all of hers.

Her doctor and I are on a first name basis on account of all the late night calls every time she twitches. In short, I've lost my damn mind. Add the fact that every time I look at her I want to bury my cock in her so deep they'd have to pry me out of there with a crowbar and you've got quite the situation.

"No, they're quiet right now, they're just missing their daddy." I reached my hand out to touch and swallowed when the hard smooth mound of her tummy moved beneath it. "See, they were waiting for your touch." She covered my hand with hers and the love swelled so huge inside me I thought I would explode.

"What's wrong, why have you been avoiding me?"

"Avoiding you?" I looked over at her sharply. If anything I would think she would be tired of me always hovering.
"Yes, you always run whenever we're alone together. The only time you're around is when the kids are there or one of the others."

"That's because I don't trust myself around you anymore." There I said it. Now she'll know her husband is a horny fuck who only thinks with his dick. She got up from her chair and came and parked her ass on my lap.

"What do you mean?" I kissed her because I couldn't help myself and ran my hand up and down her back. "I mean that when I'm around you all I want to do is make love to you and…"
"And what, you don't find me attractive anymore?" Is she fucking nuts?

"Are you bent?"
"Then why won't you touch me anymore?" She sounded like she wanted to cry and I wanted to cut my dick off. "Baby, don't cry. I don't think I could take that right now. The reason I haven't touched you is because I want you too much to hold back and I'm afraid I'll hurt you." She picked her head up and smiled at me and that sadness was gone from her eyes.

STARTING OVER

"But I'm fine. The doctor said everything's coming along beautifully and things are as they should be." I palmed her tummy and felt my babies kick against my hand. That was another problem, there was more than one of them and the asshole doctor said sometimes one hides whatever the fuck that means. Seeing that the little shits are mine they could be playing combat games in there.

Sometimes I think she can't help but be pissed at me for doing this to her, but then she's always glowing and happy and I'm left confused as fuck, because as much danger as I've faced in the zone, I couldn't do this shit no way no how.

"Let's go in I don't want you to get sick out here." There wasn't a hint of cool in the air, we were having an early spring, but this is me everyday now. Even with the kids I've grown more overprotective. Once the adoption was final and they had my name and understood the asshole spermer was a nonentity we just went all in. I was trying to make it so they never remembered his ass or that there was ever a time they had another dad other then me.

So far my son and daughter are doing just that. Everyone goes above and beyond to make sure they know that they're loved and wanted. We include them in everything especially when it comes to their siblings and now I've got Dylan as fucked up as I am when it comes to the pregnancy. He doesn't let his mom lift a finger if he's in the room. That's my boy.

I hustled her back inside and somehow we ended up in the bedroom. I used the excuse of a shower to get the salt from the pool off of me and jetted. I stayed in there way too long thinking she'd be asleep by the time I came out, but she was leaning back against the mountain of pillows looking through a magazine, waiting me out.

Dammit! I slipped on pajama bottoms and headed for the door mumbling some shit about TV. That thing she had changed into only made her tummy and tits look hot as fuck, or maybe I was just being a horn dog. The magazine hit the wall over my head and stopped me in my tracks before I reached the door.

STARTING OVER

I stopped and looked at her with my mouth open. Did she just throw that shit at me? "Oh damn baby no, what're you doing?" She was crying is what she was doing. I was at her side before the tears fell off her chin with my arms around her. "What is it?"
"You lied."
"Lied? Lied about what?" Okay just hormones we've been here before.

She pounded my chest with her little fist and I grabbed it in mine before she hurt herself. "You said you still wanted me but you lied, you can't even be in the same room." Enough of this shit! I'm not gonna have her thinking that I don't want her, that I don't find her even more desirable now than at any other time.

"So everything I said to you outside went in one ear and out the other."
"It doesn't matter what you say, I have eyes." I was slipping out of my pajama bottoms and simultaneously easing her legs open. My hands were trembling but my dick was hard and I told myself I could do this.

"Does this answer your question?" I slammed my cock into her pussy going balls deep in one stroke. "Fuck, why are you so hot, and tight and...fuck." I couldn't remember any more words in the English language so with each stroke I kept up a litany of fuck-fuck-fuck.

I covered her pregnant mound with my hand and stroked into her nice and deep. Her greedy horny ass just laid there and took it with this dreamy ass look on her face. I lifted one of her legs over my arm, opening the pussy wider so I could fuck even deeper.

Her pussy juiced like a ripe orange and sucked my shit in, massaging my dick with each thrust. "Babe shit, don't move like that." She did some sorta twist with her hips and her whole tummy shook. I was mesmerized.

"Faster Kevin, harder." She dug her heels into my ass and pulled me into her heated pussy while squeezing down around me. "I won't fuck you any harder so don't ask." But I wanted to. I wanted to pound her pussy so hard it became an obsession.

STARTING OVER

The brats in her stomach were doing somersaults or some shit and I could see them moving. That shit was keeping me in check. I ran my hand over them in awe as my dick spat pre-cum inside her and my balls drew up to my body in preparation.

I reached down and tweaked her nipples while hitting her pussy's end and she howled and came. Warm gushing juice covered my dick but she was still hungry. I pulled out and put her on her side with pillows to support her and slid in behind her. I lifted her leg up and back and forked her thighs before slipping my over hard cock deep inside her.

She liked this position because she came hard as fuck and bore down. I held her tummy in my hand and threw my head back as I off loaded deep inside her, riding out the storm as she cried out.

Once I gave in there was no stopping her and pretty soon she was riding my cock with my hands going all over her sexy as fuck body as I threw my cock up to her. I was scared as fuck when she started slamming herself down hard on my meat but there was no reining her ass in. She was on a mission.

With hands on her hips to control her movements I let her cum as much as she wanted until she tired her greedy ass out and my dick was looking for somewhere to hide, out of the line of fire. I was beat to shit but this one had enough energy to light the house.

I peeped out at her with one eye and hoped she'd had enough, damn. Her skin glowed, her hair shone and that belly was some kinda trigger, shit kept my dick hard. I finally nailed her with a hard fuck in the doggie position and that seemed to do for her. Thank fuck.

***

The one night I was too tired to think straight she would choose to go into labor. I heard the groans and the 'ouch' somewhere between sleep and wake. My hand was resting on her tummy while she slept almost sitting up with her back against my chest.

I came fully awake when her body shook in pain and damn near flew off the bed. "Okay, time, is it time?" She nodded and tried getting off the bed. I helped her up and into the shower because for some fucked up reason she decided now was a good time for a shower.

STARTING OVER

I called the doc, my sister and nosy ass Ty because he claimed Godfather rights and decided he needed to be there. Whatever, he thinks I don't know they had a bet going as to how long it would take me to level the hospital. Like I was some unreasonable asshole who couldn't handle his woman going into labor.

I got her dressed cool as a cucumber even though I was drawn tight enough to break. I got her bag outside to the truck and got the kids up. It was a toss up as to who was the most excited on the way to the hospital. I played it off but I was scared as fuck.

I barked out orders as soon as we cleared the door to the hospital. Thank fuck the others had beaten me there and took over watch of my kids so I could concentrate on their mother.

The room was already set up and they hooked her up to some Star Trek looking shit that had bells and whistles going off. At least that's what it sounded like to me.

She was holding it together pretty well which eased my fear a little but not much. I didn't like the easygoing way the staff were acting, like this shit wasn't serious. She kept apologizing to them for me whenever I'd snap at one of them when she cried out.

She'd gone behind my back and told the hack that she didn't want any drugs and had she not been a female I would've sent the doc out the fucking window each time she winced in pain. "I think we might have to go with that C-section after all." I'd read about that shit and no fucking way.

"Is something wrong with my wife, something wrong with the baby?" She shook her head no and started to explain some shit that I could give a fuck about. "Then no you're not cutting my wife so you can go play golf in an hour. Anything happens to any of them you're fucked."

She found that shit funny but I was dead ass. "Sorry but I've never found a liking for that particular sport. We talked about this Kevin. Sometimes it's easier with multiples…"
"No, is there any danger?"
"No, that's not the reason."

STARTING OVER

"Then fuck no, just get on with it." The conversation seemed surreal.

I was starting to sweat once the pushing shit started but I reminded myself that I'd been in combat before and I could do this. That shit didn't help much she was the one going through it and it was fucking with my head. "Look at me baby." She'd just had an excruciating contraction that had bent her almost double, and I almost told the doc to cut her, but I remembered her making me promise not to let them do that shit unless the babies were in danger.

She'd done everything right so there should be no problem, but now I was getting nervous. "Oh no here comes another one." She dug her nails into my hand and I gritted my teeth and endured until the pain passed and the asshole doctor kept telling her to push.

The first little cry rent the air and I watched through tear filled eyes as they passed the baby to the nurse to clean up. "You're doing good Julie, one more push for me come on." The doc kept talking which was good because I'd lost the ability. My hand had gone numb but I didn't care.

I heard their voices but nothing computed, their faces told me that everything was coming along fine. Even Julie was smiling and I wondered how the fuck she was doing that shit when she was pushing two human beings through that little hole that could barely take my cock. Good damn.

I vacillated between never breeding her again, and wanting to do that shit over and over. She looked happy, tired and weak as my second daughter came into the world. I had two of each now, maybe that would be enough.

After she was done and they'd cleaned her up I was still in a daze but joy was beginning to seep in. I held those two little beings in my arms and took them to her with more love than I ever thought possible coursing through me.

I couldn't speak so just laid them in her arms and watched them as my whole world came into focus. "How are you feeling baby?" I had to clear the frog from my throat and sit my ass down before I fell. I've never seen anything like it.

"Next time you tell me how weak you are because of your past, I'll remind you of this. Nothing that's weak can do what you just did baby. I'm in awe." I was probably fucking shit up for men everywhere but what the fuck. My baby did good. She was beaming from ear to ear.

'The good thing is, I only have to do it twice more. But if they keep coming in pairs I might get away with once." I was shaking my head before she was through. "I'm good, we're square." Fuck if I was going through that shit again. She laughed and my son opened and closed his mouth looking for the tit.

I took my little angel so her mom could feed her brother and watched as he latched on and wen to town. Like father like son. I held my daughter close and watched my wife's face. "How are you so beautiful after that shit baby?" And will there ever be a time that I don't have this burning need in me for her?

As the seconds and minutes went by the idea of planting a couple more in her was starting to look better and better. She hummed to the baby and ran her hand over his head. "He looks like you sweetie." No, he looks like a wrinkled old man. I just smiled and pretended that I could actually make out anything there but wrinkles and peeling skin.

As I sat there and the adrenaline wore off life came crashing back in. Fuck, how am I going to protect three females? At least I had my sons to help me out later, but they needed me now too. Fuck Kevin, what a bitch get your shit together.

My daughter chose that moment to open her eyes and look dead at me, as if to say 'you can do it dad.' Damn straight, I got this. First order of business. Male repellant; then a higher wall around the perimeter, more bullets, and the list goes on. "She smiled at me." My daughter smiled at me. Damn, I never knew there could be so much love in one person. My heart was full and if she wasn't already mine I would've married her again.

342 | STARTING OVER

Angel started to fuss and we switched. I held my son and silently promised that I'd always be there. Me, and his brother. We spoke softly over the babies' heads making plans, talking about the new family vehicle that should be ready soon. Regular shit! I was amazed. I've seen grown men who got grazed by a bullet act like more of a bitch. Like Tyson and his bitch ass.

"I think we better let the others in I hear Sandy's mouth." She did some shit with her hair and brushed the front of her gown and I passed her my son so that she now held them both of them again. She sniffed their heads and the doors opened letting in the family.

I got shoved out of the way while my sister and half my damn employees took over. I passed out cigars to the guys in the outer room and felt that tightness around my chest finally ease. I saw a strange woman standing in the background looking nervous as hell and didn't need an introduction to tell me who she was. Her daughter was her spitting image.

She came forward with her head bent as if expecting a blow. I waited arms folded for her to reach me. "I guess you know who I am. I'm sorry to show up here without permission. Sandy called. I asked her to." She lifted her head and there was such sadness in her eyes.

"Go meet your grandbabies." She looked like I'd just given her the key to life and bounded past me into the room where these people were making enough noise to get us kicked out of the joint.

I knew Julie would be happy to see her mom. They hadn't seen each other since she refused to see her dad and he refused to let her see her mom, who it turns out knew nothing about her kid being sold to the highest bidder.

I wasn't sure how she happened to get away to come here tonight, but if it turned out bad for her I have no problem putting a hurting on his ass. If my girl is happy to see her mom then that's what the fuck's gonna happen.

We haven't seen nor heard from the asshole since my little visit. Last I heard his dad had got him another job somewhere and he was already up to his old tricks. I didn't care one ass what that fucker did.

STARTING OVER 344

My kids never mentions him and my wife knows better. They're happy, healthy and loved. My princess came out the room looking for her daddy. She's been having some kinda abandonment issues and I can't be out of her sight for too long.

I picked her up and let her put her head on my shoulder. "Did you meet your brother and sister?"
"Yeah they're tiny daddy. I'm gonna have to take care of them." That's my girl.
"That's right princess and your little brother too." She turned up her nose. She was at that stage where females hate anything male, except her daddy and her uncle Ty of course, but we'll work on that.

Dylan came looking for me next looking war worn like he was the one who'd just gone through that shit. This kid takes the world on his shoulder but I couldn't fault him. I'm the one who's been teaching him that the women in our lives must be taken care of at all cost.

"How're you doing big brother?" He got a big smile on his face and came in for a hug. There was no uneasiness between us anymore, hadn't been for a long time.

"They're tiny dad I don't know. You think Gunner's gonna like them?" Fucking mutt will go nuts.

"Sure he will son. Just like he loves you and your sister."

I checked my watch. An hour had gone by. Time to get everyone out so my woman could get some rest. I walked back into the room where she was starting to look wilted. "Alright everybody out. Sandy the kids' bags are in the truck." She was taking them home with her for the night while I stayed here keeping watch over Julie and the babies.

They straggled out leaving me with my little family and I got to spend some time with my kids before they put them down for the night. I climbed into bed with her and held her sore body close. "Sleep baby I'm right here." She cuddled into me and sighed.

"I love you Kevin. I never get tired of hearing that shit. And even on a day like today, when she'd given me two more kids to love, nothing meant more. "I love you more."

THE END

3	**STARTING OVER**
4	
6	

Made in United States
Orlando, FL
01 April 2024